First published in Great Britain, 2024

Sunset Seduction

By Jenni Burton

Sunset Seduction

Chapter 1

Of all the hotels in all the world - she had to be sent to this one! He shook his head in sheer disbelief, a frown appearing on his forehead, his deep blue eyes narrowing darkly. Just when he needed someone to rely on, someone with plenty of experience, someone with a bit of character, someone he could trust. He'd never have chosen her – not in a million years.

'Mr Fairchild? There's a call for you, sir, from Paris.'

Greg spun round from where he had been standing, his hands in his pockets, staring out at the deep turquoise water that was the Indian Ocean. He waved to acknowledge the messenger and then walked briskly across the pool patio and into the lobby, the coolness of the air conditioning a welcome relief from the unrelenting heat outside. Glancing briefly at the reception desk that was, as ever, the centre of activity, he grimaced: this had been his main problem since arriving at the Sunset Beach Hotel barely two months ago - the lack of experienced hotel staff.

He had worked wonders in the time he had been in charge and that was not just his opinion but that of the board of the Fairfield hotel chain too. But it was not good enough, way short of his own standards and expectations and still considerably short of what his father was expecting of him. He had six months to turn this hotel around; if not, then it would close. Greg knew his reputation would nosedive with it, not only his business reputation, but his last chance of proving to his father that he was worthy of the Fairchild name, worthy of being a successor to his brother John who had died so tragically six years ago.

That was why Greg was so anxious for the new assistant manager to arrive and get settled in as soon as possible. The previous manager had, finally, put out the distress call to head office for an assistant. But by the time Greg Fairchild arrived, things had gone from bad to worse and the hapless manager had been sacked. Greg had called on head office to hurry up the new appointment, stressing that he needed someone who was particularly experienced on the leisure and entertainment side.

As he approached the hotel reception desk, Greg's frown deepened. He could hear a rising babble of noise. The phone call from Paris could well be about some new backers he was hoping to attract, and he didn't have the time to be detained. He increased his pace but was not quite quick enough.

'Oh, Homer, look, there's the manager, that nice Mr Fairchild. He'll sort us out. Coo-ee, Mr Fairchild.'

The strident tones of Mrs Mildred Armitage, with her husband dutifully in tow, rang across the hotel lobby and half a dozen other guests also turned as they noticed Greg. There was no chance that he'd be lost in the melee anyway, Greg Fairchild was rarely overlooked. At six feet, he stood a head above most of the elderly guests that the hotel was attracting at the moment, and his large frame and upright bearing marked him out as a man to be noticed. The dark brown hair, deep tan and blue eyes just added to the fact that he was a good-looking man, although some would say his features came across as rather harsh at times, particularly when that frown dug deep into his forehead.

'I'll be with you in two minutes.' Greg's strong voice cut across the cacophony and the lobby momentarily fell silent. He mimed that he had a phone call to take and escaped around the corner before Mildred Armitage could advance any further.

'Rosalie! Who's on reception duty? And where are they?'

He made an effort to keep the anger out of his voice because his secretary, inherited – like the rest of his staff – from the previous management, had a habit of collapsing in tears at the slightest hint of trouble - and there had been plenty of that in the past few weeks.

'It's Samuel, Mr Fairchild,' she almost whispered the answer. 'You know, Rani his wife is expecting their first baby. He's just gone to see her, just for a minute. It wasn't busy a moment ago.'

Greg shuddered with disbelief at what he considered to be the totally lackadaisical attitude that seemed to permeate the whole hotel, no, the whole of the Kenyan coastline. He had been trying for two months to install some sense of urgency, of responsibility, of pride even that would turn the Sunset Beach Hotel from the edge of bankruptcy into a going concern. He needed someone to train the staff, to whip them into a routine, to arrange the shifts so that the scenario being played out in reception would be a thing of the past.

Too often Greg had found the front desk in chaos - no one in charge, no system in use for booking safaris, no one willing to take on the job of organising the hotel's evening entertainment. He had tried his best but had just realised that he had to admit defeat, only to himself, of course, certainly not to anyone else.

Even before arriving, having just looked at the state of the hotel's books, he knew his time needed to be spent on more important policy matters: getting some new money into the hotel so that the buildings could be spruced up and the gardens and beach area developed. Then, he knew, he could market the resort in the right places to attract the right people.

3

But as soon as he had stepped into the place, he had realised it was being run by a bunch of amateurs.

He had hoped that head office would send him Jamie Dixon. They had worked together before, when they were both starting out on the Fairchild hotel management training scheme, and they had shared some good times at hotels in the Far East where they had been sent to learn the ropes. Jamie had done well since, rising through the company ranks, almost ready for promotion to manager, somewhere in Fairchild's world-wide chain.

But Greg had heard only last week that Jamie had suffered a skiing accident at their newest venture in Japan. He had been relieved to learn that it was not a serious accident, but a triple break of his right leg would keep Jamie Dixon out of action for at least four months and Greg had made it clear he needed someone immediately.

And now this news: that they were sending her. He hadn't had time to look through the CV they'd faxed him from head office, and he couldn't believe they hadn't been able to find someone experienced from within their own organisation, someone who knew the Fairchild ways. But, for the moment, it seemed that he was stuck with her. Short of flying out to Paris to face the board in person, he couldn't do anything about it. But he'd make sure she didn't ruin everything for him. He'd just have to keep her in check as well as the rest of the staff.

As soon as Jamie Dixon was well enough, he'd insist she leave, and that Jamie came out to join him. His frown lifted slightly as he made the decision. A smile played at the corners of his mouth as he strode into his office, kicked the door shut behind him and lifted the phone smartly. He would put up with her for the least time he needed to and then, she would be out, out of the hotel and out of his life again. This time for good.

Chapter 2

'Just look at those wonderful beaches! And the sun! We'll soon have some colour in those pale cheeks of yours!'

For what seemed liked the twentieth time on their short plane trip from Nairobi, Susannah turned to the man sitting next to her. 'But I won't be sunbathing. I shall be working.'

'Oh, you say that now, Susi. But I'll just bet that you'll be out there on those white sands with the rest of us, soaking up the sun. You did say you'd come scuba diving with me, don't forget. We have a date.'

Susannah tried hard not to let her annoyance show. He was, after all, going to be a guest at the hotel, her hotel. But her patience was wearing thin, and she certainly did not want to be bothered by this large, loud American businessman in the first week of her new job. Yes, certainly the beaches looked inviting and of course the sun was shining - they were just about to land at Mombasa on the east coast of Kenya after all. But she was here to start a new job at the Sunset Beach Hotel, a job she was looking forward to, a job that was definitely going to be a challenge, the biggest of her career.

She would need all her wits about her, and she needed no distractions, not that Clive Channing Junior the Third - was that really his name? - would have been her type had she been looking. He had settled into the seat beside her as soon they had boarded, never mind that she had carefully put her overnight bag on it in the hope that she'd have another hour or so undisturbed to arrange her thoughts. But all such plans were dashed as he casually tossed her bag into the overhead locker and sat down, leaning over her to look out of the window.

That had been his excuse more than once as they had neared the coast.

'Never been to this part of Africa before,' he had announced. But that hadn't stopped him from telling Susannah what he was expecting to see and do, particularly on safari. That had warned her not to be too explicit about her new role at the hotel which, she had just found out, was to be his hotel too, for an undefined period.

Assistant manager was what she had told him and that, indeed, was the job she had been given by the manager of the Sunset Beach Hotel, but with a very special responsibility for rebuilding the safari side of the business. That was her speciality, having been brought up on a small game park run by her father in the former Rhodesia. But that information she kept to herself, hoping she would be kept busy in the office, learning the ropes, for the time that Clive Channing Junior the Third was going to be around.

That, though, was clearly not what he intended, and he had made that very plain when he discovered where Susannah was going to be working and that she had only spent one brief holiday in this part of the country before. He might be in close proximity in this small plane, too close for Susannah's liking, but she intended putting as much space between them once they landed.

Thankfully, just as he seemed intent on leaning over yet again to admire the turquoise blue of the Indian Ocean, the captain's voice came over the intercom. 'We're about to land at Mombasa international airport, ladies and gentlemen. Please make sure you have your seatbelts fastened.'

'It's no problem, Clive, I assure you. I can manage my case fine, thank you. But I'd better go because I think there's a car waiting for me. I'll see you at the hotel.' Susannah tried to make light of the suitcase she had just retrieved from the frenzy of the conveyor belt. Hers, thankfully, had been one of the first out and she welcomed the opportunity to get away from the man who was now really beginning to annoy her.

6

She had been told that there would be a staff car and driver waiting for her so that she did not have to use the hotel's shuttle bus, and she wanted to get to the hotel and out of sight before Clive Channing could claim her acquaintance. But it wasn't only large Americans who wanted to help the pretty girl with the amber-coloured hair. Susannah knew that she looked fragile: she was 5' 6" tall but with a petite frame that seemed to make men assume she was a female in need. For that reason, she seemed destined to be at the mercy of do-gooders who could not believe she was capable of lifting a briefcase, let alone a large suitcase.

But Susannah was determined that her new life was to be different: she was not going to be taken in ever again, not by any man! He had said that she was too fond of leaning on other people - a parasite he had called her, apparently – and that she should stand on her own feet. And that was just what she was doing: total independence, even if it meant her feeling as though her arms were coming out of their sockets as she lugged her worldly belongings along the airport concourse.

She glanced back at the crowd around the luggage conveyor belts and was relieved to see that Clive Channing Junior was still awaiting his bags. He'd have to wait, anyhow, she reasoned, for the rest of the people who were en route for the Sunset Beach Hotel.

Dragging her bags through the doorway, Susannah stopped as the heat outside hit her full in the face. It was midday and the temperature had to be in the eighties. Just right for a holiday, Susannah smiled ruefully, but working in it was a different matter. She wished now that she had sought the refuge of the ladies' cloakroom for a minute or two to tidy up before meeting the staff from the hotel. But in her haste to avoid Mr Channing, that idea had been abandoned.

Quickly, she straightened her white cotton shirt and smoothed the matching skirt, thankful that neither was badly creased. She ran her fingers through her wavy, shoulder-length hair but decided against renewing her pale pink lipstick. Where was her driver and car? As her eyes searched the roadway and the car park beyond, Susannah was aware of a bus pulling up in front of her. She glanced at it and realised, with something of a shock, that it was the Sunset Beach shuttle bus, its once-bright orange and yellow paint now faded and showing signs of rust.

'That's not a very good first impression,' she muttered to herself, making a mental note to raise the subject when she had the opportunity. As assistant manager, she felt, everything that affected the guests had to be her responsibility. But she wondered, not for the first time, exactly how much influence or power was her job title going to confer?

As her mind wandered to her new job, Susannah failed to notice the bus driver waving at her. But her reverie was brought to a sudden end as a slap on her back propelled her forward, almost into the path of a car. Just as quickly, her arm was caught in a firm grasp and the familiar tones of Clive Channing Junior sounded uncomfortably close in her ear.

'Susi, Susi, careful, now. I can see you need someone to take care of you in a strange place. Come on, you were miles away. Joshua here was trying to catch your attention.'

'Oh, oh, right, thank you, Clive.' Susannah collected her thoughts and started to walk over to where the young man was now surrounded by holidaymakers. But once again she found herself in the grasp of the big American.

'Hey, no need for you to rush in there. I've got our seats organised, honey. Just let me take your bag and we'll be on our way.'

'Clive, I told you, I'm being met by a car. You go ahead and get your place in the coach," and Susannah tried, yet again, to move away. This time she succeeded but was halted in her tracks as she heard Channing's next words.

'That's what Joshua was trying to tell you, sweetheart. There is no car for you. It's been out of action for

8

a couple of weeks, apparently. Waiting for a part from Nairobi. But there's no problem. Here's the coach and I've got us the best seats! That'll give us more time to plan our trips. I'm going to make damn sure you get to know Kenya!'

'Clive,' Susannah's tone this time was more resigned than sharp. 'I keep telling you, I'm working, I won't have time …' but her words trailed off as she realised Channing was no longer with her. He had picked up her heavy case with no effort at all, stowed it in the coach's locker and was even now organising the rest of the holiday group, sweeping a path through the centre of the melee and announcing, in loud, ringing tones, 'Make way, ladies and gentlemen, please. My friend and your new assistant manager, Miss Susi!'

Chapter 3

'Miss Susannah, Miss Susannah!' The voice calling her name only just broke above the hubbub of the noise in the hotel reception and Susannah turned, gratefully, to see a young Kenyan woman desperately trying to make her way through the crowd.

The journey from the airport to the Sunset Beach Hotel had been straightforward enough, although Susannah would have preferred the opportunity to see something of the coastal region, rather than keep up yet another conversation with Clive Channing. She had expected there to be someone on the bus to welcome them to the Kenyan coast and to explain something about the hotel; that was the usual pattern on the journey from the airport. But the bus driver had merely said that he was "filling in" for the usual man and that they would soon be there.

So Susannah had found herself fending off questions about the resort from the guests in the front few rows of the bus, feeling quite inadequate to the occasion. Much to her inward annoyance, she had found herself thanking Channing when he gallantly intervened to explain that it was only "Miss Susi's" first day, and he was sure all their questions would be answered when they got to the hotel. At least that had stopped the questions coming but Susannah was cross that she - and the hotel - had been put in such an embarrassing position.

'Another thing I'll have to have a word with the manager about,' she thought. 'But where is he?' was the question going through Susannah's mind now that the bus had dropped them off and they had straggled into the hotel foyer only to find the reception desk empty and no sign of life.

'Oh, Miss Susannah, I'm so glad you're here. Jambo!' The woman finally reached Susannah's side and gave her the

Swahili welcome which Susannah returned with a quizzical smile.

'You must be Rosalie. It's lovely to meet you. But where's Mr Maringo? Everyone's asking for him and there doesn't seem to be anyone on the desk.'

Susannah strove hard to keep any note of criticism out of her voice; she wanted to make a good impression on her arrival and certainly didn't want to antagonise any of the staff. But really, it was a complete shambles in the reception hall, with the guests now beginning to complain, some of them none too quietly.

'Oh, no, it's not Mr Maringo, Miss Susannah. He's gone. We have a new manager but he's in Mombasa town today and Samuel's wife's gone into labour and there was a problem with the swimming pool this morning and …'

Rosalie finally ran out of breath and stopped in mid-sentence, her eyes filling with tears. Susannah quickly put a friendly arm round the young woman's shoulders, shielding her from some of the guests who had just realised that she was a hotel employee and had started directing their tirade against her.

She took a deep breath. 'Rosalie, don't worry. We'll get things sorted. Just tell me where the bar is. We'll get everyone in there, give them a free drink and then I'll help you sort out the accommodation. Come on, that's what I'm here for.'

Feeling far less confident than she looked or sounded, Susannah stepped quickly onto a low table, clapped her hands and called for everyone's attention. 'Ladies and gentlemen, please?'

Gradually the room fell silent.

'If you would all like to follow Rosalie to the bar …' She paused for the few cheers that went up. 'The Sunset Beach Hotel would like to welcome you with a free drink.'

There were more cheers, and Susannah could sense that people were calming down. 'Take your time, have a look round the hotel and then we'll have your rooms sorted and your luggage delivered. There'll be a cocktail party before dinner this evening when we'll be able to answer all your questions.'

Susannah finished with a big smile, belying the feeling of panic that was tying her stomach in knots. She had no idea whether the hotel put on cocktail parties for the guests, but something had to be done to calm the situation and in the absence of the hotel manager, she was, after all, the assistant manager, albeit only five minutes into her new job!

Rosalie gave her a watery smile, and Susannah wasn't at all sure that the Kenyan girl could cope with the task she had set her. She was, Susannah recalled, the manager's secretary and as such had little contact with the guests.

Suddenly, an idea came to her. 'Clive,' she called softly as the large American came into view. 'Clive, would you do me the biggest favour?' and despised herself for smiling so sweetly at the man she had minutes earlier considered a right pest.

'Anything, Susi dear, you only have to ask,' he boomed back, patting her on the shoulder.

'Can you help Rosalie get everyone settled in the bar, please? Order them drinks, on the hotel, and that'll give me time to get the reservations organised.'

'Of course, no problem. Come on, Rosalie. Let's get those cuba libres flowing!' and he swept her off, glancing back over his shoulder to wink at Susannah. 'I think we deserve our own little cocktail tonight, eh?'

Susannah just smiled in reply but realised that he was, indeed, helping her out of a spot. The hotel would probably have to stand quite a few drinks before the day was out – and that on her very first day!

'So, Rosalie, come and sit down and tell me what's happened. Where's Mr Maringo? I spoke to him on the phone only, what, a month ago? Why did he leave?'

Susannah beckoned the secretary to join her on the veranda outside the manager's office that overlooked the pools and patios: the focal point of the hotel's leisure facilities. Anyone giving it a quick glance would see two pools, shimmering in the heat of the late afternoon. A few guests were swimming lazily, stopping at the poolside bar where others were enjoying their sundowners. A few more guests sat underneath the umbrellas, at tables or on loungers. In the distance, a group of the new arrivals were wandering down through the lush gardens to step onto the white sanded beach that fringed the turquoise of the Indian Ocean.

Susannah would have loved to be doing just that, soaking her feet in the warm sea at the end of what had turned out to be an intensely hectic afternoon. The free drink for each guest had turned into quite a few by the time Susannah had worked out the booking-in system and had then found some staff to take the guests' luggage to their individual rooms and chalets. She had not even had time to find her own room yet, her luggage was still standing by the reception desk and she desperately wanted a shower. But she also wanted to reassure Rosalie that everything was going to be all right and even more, she wanted to find out why the new manager had not been around when he was most needed.

'Miss Susannah, this ok for the party?'

'Oh, Peter, that's really good.' Susannah was genuine in her praise for the poster that one of the waiters had volunteered to make, advertising that evening's welcome party.

'Put it by the reception desk, that way everyone'll see it as they come down to dinner. That's great. Thank you.'

13

Peter lowered his eyes in embarrassment and, with a quick smile at Rosalie, went off to do the new assistant manager's bidding.

'Oh, Miss Susannah, I don't know what he'll say about a party. He's really worried about money. That's why he's in town today, he's seeing some important people.'

Rosalie looked so upset once again that Susannah reached out and took her hand. She could barely be in her twenties and she looked as though she was scared stiff of her boss. Susannah would certainly give him a piece of her mind when he deigned to show up. Fancy leaving poor Rosalie in charge when there were, clearly, all sorts of staffing problems at the hotel.

'It's not your problem, it's mine.' Susannah wondered to herself again how she could sound so confident when she was really feeling so nervous. Certainly she had solved the afternoon's problem of getting the new arrivals settled in. But a cocktail party? Perhaps she had gone overboard. But in the small game park that she had grown up on with her father, they always had drinks with their guests, every evening in fact. Although to be fair, Susannah compromised, they only had a fraction of the visitors that the Sunset Beach did. What would the new manager say? Well, she would brazen it out. After all, he hadn't been here to see what there had been. She had made a decision and everything was fine now. The price of a few cocktails would surely be a reasonable price to pay for that.

Chapter 4

'Oh, so this is where the two workers are hiding. I've been looking for you. I think you deserve a reward.' The familiar tones of a certain American made Susannah jolt up from where she had been lounging on what was fast feeling like the most comfortable chair in the world.

'Clive.' Susannah's heart sank as he joined them, for he was carrying a tray laden with drinks, nuts and fruit. She had been hoping to have a word with Rosalie and then find her room for a much-needed shower and change of clothes before the cocktail party. Clive, though, seemed determined to put paid to her plans. But however much Susannah did not want to encourage his attentions, she knew she could not be rude to him, not after all his help that day.

As Clive pulled a chair alongside Susannah's, the phone in the office rang and Rosalie quickly got up to answer it. Clive leaned closer to Susannah: 'I think between us we got everything sorted, didn't we, Susi?'

'We did, Clive. I want to thank you for helping out. You didn't have to. After all, you're on holiday now. I'll certainly be letting the new manager know how valuable your assistance was.'

Susannah took the drink he was offering. 'I shall make sure that this new manager knows exactly what you did, too.'

'Oh, I don't think there's any need for that,' Susannah dismissed Clive's offer with a wave of her hand. 'After all, it is my job.'

'Yes, but where was he? No staff to welcome us, no-one to welcome you, no-one on reception, no-one to sort out the rooms. It's hardly what you call a well-run hotel, now is it? I thought that's what the new company takeover was all about, getting the hotel up to scratch.'

Channing was now in full flight and Susannah was conjuring up mental images of him really tearing into the new manager, as soon as he showed his face. She was also puzzled but was determined not to show her ignorance. She had thought the Sunset Beach was an independent hotel, but here was an American guest telling her that a new company had taken it over. She was going to have plenty of questions for the new manager when she finally met him. In the meantime, she had one persistent and vociferous admirer to deal with.

'Now, Clive, I really don't think that will do me and my reputation much good now, will it? I'm the one who's been taken on to run all that side of the hotel. I understand from Rosalie that that's why I've been brought in. He has to see to the business side of the hotel. So, please, don't say anything, Clive.'

Susannah was conscious that she was almost begging the man not to speak up on her behalf in case it antagonised her new boss. Rosalie stepped out of the office and, for the first time that day, Susannah saw a real smile on the young woman's face.

'Good news, I hope?'

'Oh, Miss Susannah, Mr Clive, it is good news. Samuel and Rani have had their baby. It's a boy!'

'Well, then let's drink to that,' Clive was quick to refill Susannah's glass.

'Do you know what they're calling him?'

'No, they haven't chosen a name yet. She was having quite a bad time during her pregnancy they didn't want to tempt fate. But Samuel says everything's ok and he'll be back to work tomorrow.'

Rosalie looked across at Susannah, having explained to her earlier that it was supposed to have been Samuel on duty on the reception desk but that when his wife had gone into labour early, he had just left. With the other reception clerk having been pressed into service on the swimming pool emergency, it was clear that the reception desk had had a bad day.

'Oh, I'm so glad,' Susannah smiled back at Rosalie. She realised how worried the Kenyan girl had been, having known Samuel's wife since schooldays. 'If he can show me the ropes on reception tomorrow, then I'm sure he can have some more time off later in the week. When is Rani coming home?'

'They don't know yet. But he would appreciate that, Miss Susannah, I'm sure.'

Rosalie gave Susannah another of her shy smiles and turned to go back into the office. 'Is it all right if I pass on the good news? The other staff will be so pleased.'

Susannah happily nodded her consent, thinking that if Samuel's recent worries were now behind him, then at least the reception desk at the Sunset Beach might be better run from now on. But she sighed as she realised that was only one of the problems facing the hotel.

Whilst sorting out the accommodation for the new arrivals, Susannah couldn't help but notice how rundown various parts of the hotel had become. The gardens were unkempt, giving the whole hotel an untidy, uncared-for feeling. The chairs, tables and loungers all needed new coats of paint, the once brightly-coloured umbrellas had faded in the sun, and no-one had up-dated the entertainment notice board for weeks: there was even a poster still proclaiming the delights of the New Year jamboree – in April!

That'll be my first job tomorrow, Susannah thought and automatically reached for the pad of paper and pencil that rarely left her side. But as she started to write, her hand was caught by that of Clive Channing.

'Now, Susi!' His tone was accusatory. 'I really do think you're going to have to learn to relax. Come on, I've brought you a drink and you've hardly touched it. I bet you didn't get anything to eat. What say I get the kitchen to bring

17

us something here, before the party? Don't suppose you'll get much time to yourself this evening.'

Susannah knew his idea made sense and that, in all reality, she would probably be busy again with the guests once the cocktail party got under way. But now she was beginning to feel that he was taking over, assuming a concern for her that would just not do.

'Clive, look. I'm really grateful for your help today. It was brilliant. But now, it's up to me. You go off and get something to eat in the restaurant and I'll see you later at the party. But I'm working now and you're not. Go on, go off and enjoy your holiday.'

Susannah's words were softened with her usual friendly smile, and it was rare for anyone to take offence at her open, easy-tempered manner. Clive Channing smiled ruefully. 'I know, I'm getting my marching orders.' He got up and, before Susannah realised his intent, leaned over and gave her a kiss on the cheek.

'I think you've done a brilliant job today, Susi dear.' He spoke enthusiastically. 'Quite brilliant. Drinks on the house and a cocktail party: no better way to greet your guests. I hope you've started the way you mean to carry on!'

'And I sincerely hope she hasn't!' Susannah's head shot up and Clive stumbled over the table as a sharp, imperious and decidedly irate voice interrupted the moment. They turned towards the office door where a man had appeared, hands on hips and a look of pure thunder across his face.

'I go away for a few hours and what do I find when I get back? No staff on duty, my secretary gossiping on the phone, free drinks and a free cocktail party, and my new staff drinking on duty and canoodling in my office!'

He strode forward and pulled a chair out of his way, his eyes firmly fixed on Susannah's pale face. 'I expected better of you this time, Susannah.'

18

'Hey, just a minute. You have no idea what's been going on round here today.' Clive Channing recovered the first, regaining his balance and moving to stand opposite the other man. They were of a similar height and build and as they stood there, both glowering, it looked to Susannah as though they were squaring up to each other, over her! She was still reeling from the shock of seeing who the other man was: clearly the hotel manager and her new boss, but surely not him?

'Oh, I think I've a pretty good idea. Susannah and I are no strangers to each other. Or didn't she tell you that?' He turned to stare at her. 'Bringing your boyfriend along wasn't part of the job. Anyone with any sense of responsibility would know that.'

'Now, look here.' Clive's face reddened.

'No, you look here. This is my office, and Susannah is my new assistant. On her first day, I certainly expected a lot better. So I'd appreciate it if you would leave your girlfriend to do her job. I assume you have accommodation elsewhere? Because there's no way I want you hanging around the hotel …'

'Greg.' Susannah eventually found the strength to utter his name, a name that had not passed her lips for five years. It came out low and unintentionally husky. Both men turned to look at her.

'Well?' Greg opened his mouth, clearly intending to let off another tirade but Susannah forestalled him by getting to her feet and putting a comforting hand on Clive Channing's arm.

'Let me introduce you. Clive, this is Greg Fairchild, obviously the new manager of the Sunset Beach Hotel. Greg, this is Clive Channing Junior the Third, a guest at your hotel. We both arrived today, and Clive has been extremely helpful …'

It was the expression on Greg's face that made her stop in mid-sentence. He looked, for a fleeting moment, quite devastated and, if she had not known him better, almost embarrassed.

'Oh, my … Clive! I do apologise. I was hoping to be back in time to welcome you to the hotel. But you know how it is, I just got held up in meetings in Mombasa all day long. Look, let's have a drink before dinner and perhaps you'd like to join me for dinner too, to make up for the misunderstanding.'

Within seconds, Greg had changed from raging boss to efficient businessman, effectively excluding Susannah from the scene. The two men shook hands, and Clive seemed content to be led back into the office, pausing momentarily to turn to wink at Susannah.

As they left the veranda, she sank back into the chair and took a much-needed gulp of the fruit punch that Clive had provided. It just couldn't be him! It was supposed to be Mr Maringo. That's who she had spoken to on the phone, that's who she'd been expecting. He was an old friend of her college professor's, and it was through their acquaintance that she had landed the job. He'd been impressed by the fact that she was an experienced safari leader, that she spoke Swahili and that she had had some, albeit brief, experience working with a hotel chain, the Fairchild Corporation.

So what was Greg Fairchild doing here? Surely a small, ailing hotel like this couldn't interest the heir to one of the world's leading leisure companies? She would have thought he was at least a director by now, based in Paris or New York or London, not hidden away from the glamour of the big time. He had had big plans back them. It was clear that he was going places and that she wasn't good enough to be part of that future, that her father's game park was only small-time and that she had no idea of what the leisure industry was all about.

20

So why here? How were they going to work together, after all that had passed between them? Should she give in now? He probably wouldn't be at all surprised if she handed her resignation in tonight and got on the first plane in the morning. But where could she go?

Chapter 5

On her father's death only three months ago, she had been shocked to learn that the game park on which she had grown up was not to be hers after all. Her father had, apparently, got further and further into debt as the tourist industry waned with the periodic outbreaks of violence in the country and he had secretly sold out to a local businessman, a man whom Susannah had known most of her life as a good neighbour. He had allowed Susannah barely a week to grieve before claiming his property.

He had offered her a job: firstly, as his mistress and then as a waitress. So Susannah had had no alternative but to pack her bags and leave, seeking shelter with her old zoology professor in Harare. It was he who had recognised her need to get a job and regain her independence and he who had phoned his friend Mr Maringo.

As Susannah came back to the question that had been bothering her all day, just what had happened to Mr Maringo, her thoughts were interrupted by the sound of footsteps. Now, perhaps, she would get some answers. This time, she would not let Greg Fairchild have the last word. She was going to stand by everything she had done today and prove to him that she could do the job. Small time, indeed! Just who did he think he was?

'Well, Susannah. Clive's been telling me what happened when you arrived. Unfortunately, that's exactly the sort of thing I've had to deal with ever since I arrived: poor staff, no sense of responsibility. It's hopeless.'

'Is that an apology, Greg? Because I think I deserve one, a proper one!' Susannah could not believe those words had come out of her own mouth. Never had she spoken to anyone like that, least of all the great Greg Fairchild, heir to the Fairchild Corporation. Her new found determination was clearly working. She glanced up at Greg's eyes and saw a flicker of amusement.

'Susannah.' His tone was one of enforced patience. 'We have to work together. It may be only temporary, but I think we should at least try to get on. I gather you did a good job today and I'm willing to give you credit for that.'

'Big of you,' Susannah thought but kept it to herself.

'Maybe promising a cocktail party was the only thing you could think of in the circumstances. So, we'll go ahead with it. After all, if you promise something, you really should deliver!'

This time, the look in his eyes was definitely more than mere amusement, more like devilment and Susannah reacted. Her right hand came up in a swift movement, aiming for his cheek. But Greg was too quick for her. His hand caught her wrist and held it, not tightly but firmly, as he placed his other hand under her chin.

'Quite the little firebrand now, aren't we? You've certainly changed, Susannah. You were never this animated, if I remember. Quite a shy, reserved young thing, weren't you? Or was that just a front?'

'How dare you! Let me go!'

'I will when you've calmed down. I don't think attacking your new boss is the best way to begin, do you?'

Susannah stared back at him without moving.

'Now I admit that we haven't got off to the best of starts. But we have an awkward situation here and you are going to have to help me out. I'm willing to let bygones be bygones and we'll start with a clean slate. Ok?'

'Ok.' Susannah gritted her teeth and he slowly let his hands fall to his side, never taking his eyes off her face.

'I need an assistant manager and you, I believe, have experience of safaris, yes?'

She nodded.

'So, let's see how things work out for a couple of months. I'm sure we can be polite with each other, in public at least, for that long, can't we?'

'Yes.'

'So, you just do your best. Get the reception desk properly manned, get the safaris organised, keep the staff and the guests off my back and I'll give you a good reference. Can't say fairer than that, can I? After all, it'll be great experience for you, after your family's little outfit, won't it?'

'You patronising bast …' Susannah's outraged reply was cut short as Greg's hands regained hold of her wrist and chin and he bent his head towards hers.

'Just for old time's sake …' Susannah just caught the dangerous twinkle in his eyes before she felt his lips on hers and for a second, she could do nothing to resist, just accept the pressure from his mouth as it bore down, relentlessly.

'Oh!' Susannah quickly discovered that this was exactly the wrong word to utter as Greg's mouth only clamped harder on her own and, with her lips parted, his tongue forced its way, insistently, inside. For a moment, the sensation took Susannah back five years, to the time when she had welcomed such intimacies. But it only took a second for her to realise that this was, indeed, five years on and that the man now kissing her was a fraudster, a liar and not really interested in her, only in another scalp.

As he carried on kissing her, Greg had released his grip on Susannah, moving his hands to pull her closer towards him. But he soon realised his mistake as her well-aimed right palm hit him squarely on the cheek. Before he could react, she moved out of his reach. At that moment, there was a sound from the office and Rosalie appeared, timidly putting her head round the door.

'Ehmm, Mr Fairchild, Miss Susannah, I'm sorry to disturb you …'

'What is it, Rosalie?' Greg's tone was curt as he turned his back on her to stare out at the swimming pools.

'I'm sorry, sir. It's just that Peter wants to know what drinks to serve at the cocktail party. Only, some of the guests are turning up early and he doesn't know whether you want him to serve spirits or ...'

'It's Miss Susannah's party, Rosalie. Ask her.'

Susannah stared at the broad back that was all she could see of Greg. Her hand was still stinging from the slap she had given him, and she was sure that his cheek would bear the imprint. Much as she would have liked to see his discomfiture made public, she realised that maybe that particular pleasure would not serve her own best interests in either the short or long term.

'Rosalie, I'll deal with that. Come on, I'll see Peter and then I must have just five minutes to make myself presentable.'

Susannah forced herself to laugh light-heartedly as she ushered the young woman back into the office. Before she left the veranda though, she spoke in lower tones to Greg, still standing with his back to her. 'I expect you to do your bit tonight, Greg. The guests are so anxious to meet their manager, although I can't imagine why!'

Greg almost turned at Susannah's heavily sarcastic tone but just managed to stay where he was as she continued.

'As you're the one who's so keen on public relations, I think this should be your show. Keeping the guests happy is what hotels are about, Greg. Not just making money. But perhaps that's where we differ? I don't think you've ever cared for the guests, have you? They're just numbers on a spreadsheet to you, aren't they? Well, they're not to me, they're people wanting a new experience, whether it's a party of four at my father's camp or ...'

Susannah's breath caught in her throat and she was unable to continue, as the realisation came home to her that it hadn't been her father's camp, that he was no longer there for her to turn to and that she had to make a new life for herself. At this moment that new life was here, as assistant to a man who clearly didn't trust or respect her. She turned away before Greg could see the tears that were welling in her eyes. She was tired, she rationalised. It had been a hell of a day, and she needed a shower. Then, perhaps, she would be able to cope better with this man from her past who was definitely not going to get the better of her in the future.

Chapter 6

'No, Clive, I don't think that's a good idea. I'm sure Greg will say a few words and then the evening can just start. I really don't think …"

But whatever Susannah had or had not been thinking was lost on the American who was already halfway across the dance floor. When Clive Channing Junior the Third strode purposely, anywhere, people took notice. Groups of guests who had been happily chatting over drinks gradually fell silent and the band, who had been playing background music, stopped in mid-flow. Susannah looked around, helplessly, for Greg.

Since leaving his office in tears after their earlier encounter, she'd stayed well out of his way. She had finally found her room, had made a half-hearted attempt at unpacking and then had tried to relax for all of five minutes in the shower before dressing for the cocktail party.

Much to her amazement, it was going extremely well. She and Greg had, mutually, avoided each other. To anyone observing them, their behaviour exactly conformed to the Fairchild Leisure Group management training guidelines: each making sure they mixed with as many guests as they could, each joining in conversations, each partaking of just one drink themselves, politely declining any more.

When the dinner gong sounded, Susannah had disappeared into the kitchen, on the pretext of introducing herself to the staff there. She spent the time talking to the chefs, waiters and helpers, asking them about their work schedules, picking at a starter, declining the main course of Indian curry and snatching half a fruit salad before emerging, carefully, into the lounge and ballroom area.

That was when she had been pounced upon by the other man she was anxious to avoid, this time to no avail.

'Ladies and Gentlemen.' Clive's voice boomed out over the band's main microphone. 'Ladies and Gentlemen!'

Even the bar staff and waiters stopped in mid-action as Clive upped the decibels. This time, the effect was instantaneous. He had everyone's attention, and he seemed, to Susannah, to be perfectly at ease in front of perhaps hundred or so people.

'I'm sure you'd like to join me in thanking the Sunset Beach management for an excellent party tonight.'

If Susannah had been hoping to maintain a low profile that evening, then she realised that this was now totally out of the question. For Clive was waving expansively in her direction and loud applause had her blushing furiously. To add to her confusion, she suddenly realised that someone else had appeared at her side, to the accompaniment of yet more handclapping.

'What is going on?' Greg's words were muttered, exasperatedly, in her ear.

'I don't know. I couldn't stop him. He's your friend,' she replied indignantly.

'You're the entertainment manager. You do something,' came the sharp retort.

Tired, hungry and emotional, Susannah turned to face her adversary. Oblivious to their guests and to the next part of Clive's speech, she opened her mouth to tell Greg exactly what she thought of him, but was forestalled as he took her arm, none too gently, and firmly pushed her onto the dance floor.

'What are you doing?' She tried to pull back, but Greg's grasp was unyielding.

'Smile.' The order came through gritted teeth as Greg put on the public smile she knew so well. Aware now that they were in full view of everyone, Susannah could do nothing but obey his command.

As she looked around, she realised that people were smiling at them. Then she caught the end of Clive's announcement: '... so our manager Greg Fairchild, and our lovely new assistant manager, Miss Susi, will show you all the way by leading off the dancing this evening.'

Greg let out a swear word which, luckily, was drowned out by the band starting up. He released his grip on her arm but, before Susannah could move away, pulled her back even closer, his right hand tightly clasping her left, his left hand going around her waist to rest in the small of her back.

'Dance, dammit!' was his next order and Susannah found herself pressed firmly against the length of his body as he swept her into a lively waltz. Against her will, Susannah found herself moving easily around the dance floor. She had forgotten what a good dancer Greg was or had been five years ago. Dancing lessons had been a compulsory part of the Fairchild training scheme: staff were expected to join in all their guests' activities and Greg had picked her as his partner right from the start. Susannah hadn't had much call for ballroom dancing on her father's game reserve. But Greg Fairchild, or Greg Chambers as he'd called himself then, had been the most accomplished dancer on the course. He'd been only too willing to teach Susannah to dance to his tune.

'At least look as though you're enjoying yourself.' Greg's voice sounded in her ear, his mouth hovering dangerously close.

Susannah tried again to pull away but found herself imprisoned. She looked up, saw the familiar twinkle in his eyes and realised that he was enjoying her discomfort.

'I trust we're not going through this charade every evening?' she queried, treating him to her most winning public smile.

'Who knows? Depends on whether your beau carries on like this.' Greg was opening laughing now.

'He is NOT my beau!' Susannah hissed back.

'Susannah,' Greg lowered his head so that their eyes were barely inches apart. 'Remember our pact. Be civil to each other in public. We want the guests to think we're a team, running a great hotel. So, please, for once, relax. It's just one dance.'

He pulled her closer still. The dance seemed to go on forever. Susannah tried to keep her face averted from Greg's: his mouth was definitely too close for comfort and his hands felt as though they were all over her body. Even worse was that he seemed totally at ease and enjoying every second. The thought annoyed Susannah and for a second she missed her footing, accidentally clipping Greg's ankle with her sandal. She felt him wince and then pull her closer.

'You used to be such a good dancer,' he whispered.

'Oh, I had a good teacher,' she replied, her voice heavy with sarcasm.

'Not much practice since, eh?'

Susannah very nearly kicked him again, although this time it would have been done on purpose, but at that moment, the waltz finished and the band neatly slid into a quickstep. Susannah tried to pull away but Greg's grasp stayed firm.

'Now, now. It'll look as though we don't like each other,' he grinned down at her. 'Just one more, then we'll both get back to work.'

'This IS work. It's certainly not pleasure!' Susannah had to lower her voice as some of the guests had taken the floor and were now dancing close to them. Greg laughed out loud and neatly swung her through a turn.

'Oh, Susannah, you really haven't changed, have you? You always did divide everything up into neat little compartments, didn't you? This is work time; this is playtime and never the twain shall overlap. That's what you said, but we both know you didn't practise what you preached, don't we?'

His voice had become low and serious, and his left hand moved from her waist up to her neck, forcing her to look at him.

'I don't know what you're talking about,' Susannah's reply was indignant.

'Oh, come on.' Greg had dropped his false smile now and was staring down at her, hostility in his deep blue eyes.

'I have no idea what you're on about.' Susannah's voice was rising.

'Now, now, now. Looks like this is just the right time for me to cut in.' Clive Channing appeared between them, smiling broadly. 'Can't keep her to yourself all night, now, Greg. That wouldn't be playing fair, now would it? I think there's a little lady over there who particularly wants to dance with you.'

Neatly for such a large man, Clive insinuated himself between the two of them, taking Susannah's hands in his and leading her a yard or so away from the immobile Greg.

'Oh, coo-ee, Mr Fairchild. I know it's a gentleman's excuse me, but just this once, could I have the pleasure?' and Mrs Mildred Armitage giggled coyly as she joined Greg on the dance floor.

Susannah couldn't help but smile at the expression of outrage on Greg's face which he quickly masked, not altogether successfully. She turned to Clive. 'Thank you. I'd be delighted to dance with you,' she said, loudly enough for Greg to hear. He spun on his heels and took hold of the matron, leading her off into a lively, if silent, quickstep, but with a backward glance at Susannah that said all too clearly that he had plenty more to say to her.

Chapter 7

As he sipped his coffee by the swimming pool, Greg couldn't help but reflect on the previous evening. In truth, he admitted to himself, he was still in a state of shock. Not that anyone else would ever have the slightest inkling. Greg was proud that he could keep his innermost feelings safely hidden from public gaze. But underneath, he was still reeling from the effect Susannah was having on him, after all this time.

After just hours at the hotel, she had organised a most successful cocktail party that had got many of the guests talking to each other for the first time since he had taken over. This morning, he had discovered that the flowing of free drinks at the cocktail party had actually resulted in more than doubling the usual sales of drinks for the rest of the evening. He wouldn't tell Susannah that, he decided. She would only say that he was totally money-oriented. But that was his job, after all. She was responsible for looking after the guests; his job was to see that the hotel stopped losing money.

After just one evening, it appeared that they might have found the perfect partnership. Partnership! Greg's laugh was harsh. But then he recalled how they had danced together, at Channing's insistence, and how feelings he thought long buried, had resurfaced. Holding Susannah in his arms had once again been an exceptionally pleasant experience. Her head fitted so comfortably against his cheek, her hair was soft against his skin, her body fitted so neatly against his ...

He got up quickly, crashing his coffee cup back onto the saucer, and moved away from the public pool area. He strode towards the wooded area that fringed the beach. Whenever he needed to sort out a problem, and there had already been a fair few of those in his few months at the hotel, he had found walking in the cool of the palm trees helped. Not that the problems had been sorted - yet. But the walk always seemed to calm him down, so that he could analyse situations more rationally. More than once in recent weeks, he had decided he was getting old.

'You uscd to be able to make instant decisions, Fairchild!' He had chastised himself. 'It must be age getting to you if it needs a walk in the woods to make up your mind.'

But the habit had developed and now Greg found himself wandering deep in thought, the sounds of the hotel gradually receding into the distance. Reluctantly, and not knowing quite why he felt compelled to do so, he found himself looking back over his adult life. His thoughts went back to his student days. He'd been a bright enough scholar, but he'd never had the dedication to studying that his older brother, John, had shown. John went to Cambridge; Greg to a red-brick university. John graduated with a First; Greg spent his time excelling at sport and socialising; in between, he just scraped a 2.2 degree.

He could still remember his father's words to him at the time: 'You never were as clever as your brother. Still, I expect we can find you a place in the firm.'

Greg declined that offer with the family concern: the Fairchild Corporation was a small but expanding hotel company at the time. He packed his bags and left, embarking on a happy-go-lucky life, at first financed by a family trust fund that had come to him on his 21st birthday. Then, finding his feet in the business world, he spent his time wheeling and dealing in the stock markets, making small fortunes and spending them. Tall, goodlooking and a free spender, he was never short of female companionship and never felt the need to single out one and settle down.

He travelled the world many times over, joining the jet sets at all the top resorts: Monte Carlo, Rio, Paris, London. Relations with his father remained distant. Greg dutifully turned up at the expected family gatherings: Christmas, cousins' weddings and christenings. But Greg always felt his father's disappointment in his younger son, showering his affection, instead, on John. Their mother had died when the boys were at boarding school in their early teens and consequently neither had ever enjoyed a really close family feeling. The brothers had been thrown together and, despite the rift between Greg and Fairchild senior, the brothers' teenage friendship endured.

John, whenever business permitted, joined Greg on holidays in the Caribbean and the Far East and the two had a good time: chasing women, soaking up the sun and enjoying life to the full. But everything changed for the Fairchild family six years ago when John was killed in a car crash, whilst taking part in a car rally in Uganda. Their father was devastated as was Greg, but neither felt able to share their grief.

For Greg, it had been a turning point. He had spent time with John before the accident and they had talked about their father. John was adamant that he loved his sons equally, but that he just couldn't put it into words; a bit like Greg himself, he had ventured. Greg hadn't paid much attention at the time. But after the funeral, he thought back to his brother's words and decided to make the first move.

He told his father that he did, after all, want to join the Fairchild Corporation, to help take the place of his brother. He knew as soon as the words were out of his mouth that he hadn't phrased it right, but he wasn't prepared for his father's harsh response. 'You can never replace your brother,' he was told. 'But if you want to join the firm, then you start as an ordinary trainee. You'll get no favours from me!'

'I wouldn't want any,' Greg retorted and immediately went off to make arrangements with the head of personnel to join the latest intake of management trainees, under an assumed name.

Greg had spotted Susannah on the first day of the course. The new recruits were gathered in the lounge of one

34

of the Fairchild's older hotels on the outskirts of London and were awaiting the arrival of the course leaders. Greg stood apart from the rest in one corner of the room, silently assessing his fellow trainees. He wasn't sure what he had let himself in for, but he was determined that he would succeed and on his own merits. His father's parting words still rang in his ears: 'You can never replace your brother. I doubt you've got what it takes.'

'Hi, I'm Robyn. I'm guessing from the look on your face that you don't rate this place much, either. Quaint, ain't it?'

Greg's thoughts were interrupted by the ringing tones of a tall, statuesque young woman. He almost winced at her use of the word quaint but then remembered that, to all intents and purposes, he was just like her: a newcomer to the Fairchild Corporation, just finding his feet.

'Hello. Yes, amazing isn't it?'

'Well, that's one word for it,' Robyn laughed loudly. 'I just hope I don't end up in a place like this. I joined for a future, not to live in the past.'

Greg forced a smile to his lips. Mustn't alienate his fellow students, he thought. After all, they were going to be in each other's company for the next two months.

'And you are?' Robyn's prompt reminded him of his new persona.

'Greg.' He held out his hand. 'Greg Chambers. Good to meet you.'

'Well, Greg. I'm sure I don't think much of the Fairchilds so far.' Robyn's voice echoed across the room and a number of the other trainees turned to look at her.

'What? What do you mean?' For a moment Greg thought he'd been found out and that she was referring to him. But her next words banished his worries.

35

'This!' She flung her arms expansively around at the group. 'Hardly good management practice, is it? What? Twenty, no, nearly thirty minutes late on the first day.'

Several other people nodded in agreement and moved over to join them. Robyn continued her diatribe, clearly relishing being the centre of attention.

Greg found himself caught: he disliked hearing the Fairchild Corporation criticised, but he realised that, to the newcomers, their first impressions hadn't been the best. As Robyn warmed to her theme, Greg edged to the back of the group. He looked around and noticed that another of the trainees, a young woman, had not joined the admiring throng, but was talking to a waiter just outside the lounge door.

As he approached, he heard her say: 'Would it be possible for us to have coffee now, please? I understand the course leaders have been delayed and I think we were due to have a coffee break quite soon anyway. It'll save time. But only if that's convenient for you?'

A smile accompanied the request, and the waiter quickly returned with a trolley, laden with coffee and biscuits.

'What a good idea.' Greg quietly congratulated the young woman as she started pouring the drinks. She looked up briefly and there was that smile again.

'Well, it'll stop them moaning for a while, won't it?' nodding her head in the direction of Robyn and the others.

'I'm Greg … Chambers,' he introduced himself, again finding his assumed name difficult to remember. For a moment, a feeling of guilt washed over him. But almost immediately he knew that it had to be this way; what would be the reaction of the other students had he announced who he really was?

'Hello, Greg,' the young woman's voice was soft. 'I'm Susannah. Would you like some coffee?'

Greg nodded and, much to his own surprise, found himself adding: 'Here, let me help.'

Once the coffee had been distributed, Greg had deliberately taken a seat on the far side of the room, just so that he could observe Susannah during the introductory session that followed.

Understated. That's what she was he decided. She was understated in almost every way. As each of the trainees was asked to introduce themselves, he noted that her voice was soft and gentle but somehow, at the same time, quite decisive, not submissive by any means. Her own resume had been concise and the information that she had been brought up on a game park in Rhodesia explained the honey-coloured tan that he found so attractive.

But it was her hair that fascinated Greg. Shoulder length, neatly cut in a bob, it was the colour of fine sand, lightened here and there, he guessed, quite naturally by the sun. He'd been so absorbed in watching her that he had almost been caught out by the course leader asking him for his background. He had a story prepared, of course, but once again that feeling of guilt washed over him as he informed his fellow trainees that after graduating, he had worked in a number of hotels around the world in a variety of jobs, leaving them to imagine him as an itinerant barman and waiter.

He almost held his breath when he finished, wondering whether anyone was about to unmask him as an impostor and a Fairchild. But his manufactured story was as unremarkable as many of the others and the course leader soon passed on to the next trainee.

Chapter 8

Over the next few weeks, the group got to know all about the Fairchild Corporation and more about each other. In all the exercise activities, Greg was a popular co-worker: his easy outgoing manner attracted many of the women; his ability to mix in all company was noted by the trainers and they soon realised he had a natural tendency towards leadership, which even the other males did not resent, despite the competitive nature of the course.

Greg struck up a friendship with a young man from Australia, Jamie Dixon. At first, he'd been wary of sharing heart-to-hearts with any of the others, just in case they put two and two together and somehow recognised him. But Jamie, he soon realised, was young, naive and not well travelled, having only ever worked in a couple of small hotels on the outskirts of Melbourne and then Sydney. He hadn't mixed in any of the company that Greg had been part of when he'd visited the Antipodes for Melbourne Cup race day, the Sydney-to Hobart yacht race and various top tennis and golf tournaments, all part of the jet-setters' calendar.

But while he might drink with Jamie in the hotel bar late into the evening - when the trainers had long since departed for their own homes - Greg found himself far more interested in keeping a close eye on Susannah. She intrigued him. During the days, she took part competently in all the training exercises, learning quickly, never showing off, assisting the others, contributing to any group activity. But she was not one of the more vociferous of the group. She let the others do the talking, the discussing and, at times, the arguing, and then gave her opinion in a measured, considered way.

After a while, Greg began to think that what he had taken for intrigue was, in fact, a lack of passion. But in their group exercise the following day, he'd been surprised and pleased to be proved wrong when she had put up a spirited and knowledgeable defence when Robyn had launched a stinging criticism about restricting wild animals to safari parks. When Susannah realised that she was the centre of the group's attention, she blushed a charming pink and even started apologising to the Robyn for her outburst.

But Greg defended her and even Robyn acknowledged Susannah's undoubted expertise in the field. As the training session packed up that evening, Greg was determined that Susannah was not going to slip away to her room, as she had done every night so far. As she struggled to close down the flip chart their group had been using, he offered dinner in exchange for his help.

Smiling, she gave in. 'I don't know why these things are so awkward,' she said. 'They're clearly made for people your height.'

She hadn't been prepared, though, for Greg to appear for their date in an overcoat. 'Aren't we staying here?'

'It's great food and I'm just as much a fan of the Fairchild Corporation as you, but I just fancy a change,' he replied. 'How about Chinese?'

'Oh, yes,' Susannah's grin was infectious and they enjoyed their escape from the Fairchild establishment, eating at a run-down, but genuine Chinese restaurant in the nearby town.

One aspect of his former life that Greg refused to give up when he began the course was his car, his pride and joy - a Porsche. He'd initially been disappointed when Susannah merely complimented him on it and his driving. He was much more used to the women who'd passed through his life being gushing in their praise for so sporty and expensive a car. But as the evening had gone on, he realised that Susannah was not at all impressed by wealth and material assets.

His plan had been to take her to a Chinese restaurant that he'd been recommended by friends with royal connections. But she was the one who'd chosen a rather seedy-looking restaurant, persuading him that it was always worth eating at a restaurant where the Chinese themselves ate. She was right. Totally unpretentious, clean and friendly, it was just the right setting for their first date, although he wasn't sure that that was how Susannah regarded their evening together.

When the bill came, she insisted, quietly but quite determinedly, that they split the cost. Knowing how much he had in the bank at the time, and guessing a little at Susannah's situation, Greg tried to dissuade her. But when a shadow fell across those green eyes, albeit ever so briefly, he gave in gracefully.

When they returned to the hotel, Susannah declined the offer of a night-cap but allowed Greg to escort her to her door. There, she had offered her hand, thanking him for the evening. Possibly for the first time in his life, Greg had settled for a woman's handshake, going off to bed bemused at his own behaviour and his feelings.

Robyn made several attempts to engage Greg's attention over the next few weeks, but all failed. He found, initially much to his surprise, that the openness and confident brashness that he had once found attractive in the opposite sex, now repelled him. It was increasingly Susannah's company that he sought after each day's training, whether to sit quietly in a corner of the lounge, gently discussing the course and occasional snippets of their personal lives, or exploring the local countryside in his sports car, and enjoying the occasional drink in one of the many delightful pubs that dotted this area of Kent.

As their first month drew to a close, tension amongst the trainees began to mount, because they had been told in no uncertain terms that anyone not up to scratch would be leaving the course before the next stage. Greg found Susannah quite agitated one evening when he had gone to look for her.

40

'I don't know that I'm suited to this,' she burst out, in a rare moment of personal candour. 'It's not me, dressing up and acting a part. I can't do it!'

Greg took her in his arms and held her close, recognising that she was close to tears but desperately not wanting to give way in front of him. All day they had been role-playing and Greg had noticed Susannah's increasing discomfiture. In everything else on the training course, she excelled. But it was clear to everyone, fellow trainees and course leaders alike, that she had no liking or aptitude for acting out a part.

'That's what we really are,' Robyn had insisted. 'We're all playing a part, whether we like it or not. That's what the Fairchild Corporation want us to do and that's what they reckon our hotel guests want. We're none of us acting ourselves. Isn't that right, Greg?'

Once again Greg felt a flash of guilt course through his body, fear at being unmasked. His instinct was to glance at Susannah. He realised that his feelings for her were growing stronger and that, if reciprocated, he would have to come clean at some stage. But he wanted to do it in his own time, of his choosing, rather than be unmasked in front of everyone.

This time, though, Robyn was only commenting on the public persona that Fairchild employees were expected to show to each and every hotel guest - of the calm, competent, utterly professional Fairchild employee.

'They'll tell me I'm not suitable. I know they will,' Susannah's voice was breaking and she struggled out of Greg's grasp. 'I might as well pack it in now. I'm not like Robyn. I can't sing, I can't dance, I can't talk like she does ...'

'Thank goodness for that.' Greg pulled her back into his arms, this time forcing her to face him. 'I'm sure the Fairchild Corporation will find something quite suitable for

Miss Robyn Jackman to do,' he said, pulling Susannah closer. 'She could always be the pool cabaret on our cruise ship!'

His words produced a half-hearted smile from Susannah: Robyn's dislike of water had been well-aired over the past few weeks. And that was all the encouragement Greg needed. He bent his head and, not feeling any resistance, kissed Susannah on her half-parted lips. At first he felt no response, just a second of mere compliance. But then she returned the pressure, and their lips parted. All Greg was conscious of was the smell and the taste of her, a heady mixture of subtle perfume and the cool, sensuous honey of her mouth.

A low moan escaped from Susannah's lips and Greg reluctantly pulled back, gazing into her eyes which were still brimming with tears. 'Susannah?' He whispered her name and pressed his lips to her forehead. He wanted to hold her even more tightly but was scared she might push him away. For the first time in his life, Greg discovered, he was fearful of a woman's reaction. But not any woman. This was Susannah. He wanted her, for keeps.

'Greg? Are you there? We're off down the pub. You coming?' The strident voice of Jamie Dixon echoed across the lounge.

Greg and Susannah jumped away from each other, Susannah turning to stare out of the window, wiping her eyes. Greg ran his fingers through his hair and turned to face the newcomer.

'Jamie, hi. I'll meet you down there, later. OK?'

He tried to shield Susannah from the young man's view but wasn't successful.

Oh, Susannah,' Jamie's voice was flat. 'Not still upset, are you? Role playing is just not your thing, is it?'

'Jamie!' Greg took a step towards him. 'Leave her alone, will you? We've all had a long day and remarks like that

42

don't help. We're going to have a quiet coffee here and I may see you at the pub later. OK?'

This time the query was more of a command and Jamie heard the rebuke in Greg's voice.

'Sorry, Susannah. I didn't mean any harm. We can't all be Robyn Jackmans, can we?'

'Jamie!' Greg was getting exasperated at the young man's heavy-handed attempts to get back in favour. He'd noticed that Jamie had tried to chat Susannah up on several occasions in the past few weeks and had been politely rebuffed each time. He was far too young, naive and gauche for someone like her, Greg reasoned to himself. But thanks to Jamie's untimely interruption, Greg had still to find out if he was the one for Susannah.

'No, it's all right. You go,' Susannah's words were low. 'I'm all right, really.'

But the look in her eyes said the opposite and Greg waved the other man away.

'Go, Jamie. I'll come for a drink another night. Not now.'

Neither Greg nor Susannah noticed Jamie leave; they were only conscious of each other.

Greg sighed as he realised that the feelings he'd had back then were just the same as he'd experienced last night, dancing with Susannah. Sure, she had held herself stiffly in his arms, clearly determined not to get an inch closer to him than was strictly necessary. But they had glided round the dance floor together, their steps matching completely, as though the intervening five years had not existed.

Physically, yes, they were a match and again a sigh escaped from Greg's lips. For a second, he contemplated rushing headlong into the Indian Ocean: no dramatic gesture, just the equivalent of a cold shower. But then he thought of what had happened after that evening all those years ago now.

43

How she had led him on, promising everything with her eyes, but not delivering.

It was just as well that Jamie Dixon had told him that she had known all along that he was a Fairchild. Apparently she had even boasted to the others that she was going to snare him and the Fairchild fortune. The night Jamie told him, there was a crisis at the hotel, a burst water pipe or something, Greg couldn't rightly remember. By the time it was all over, he had glimpsed Susannah stealing out of the door. The others were informed that there had been a family emergency. Greg didn't believe it. She'd gone because she'd been found out. And he had had a lucky escape!

Chapter 9

The hotel was quiet; the quietest it had been since she'd arrived. Susannah allowed herself a congratulatory smile. Right at this moment, everything was going to plan. Her efforts over the past three weeks were beginning to pay dividends: a quiet hotel was an organised hotel, the first sign that some order had been introduced into the chaos that had been the Sunset Beach.

More than half the guests had taken up one of Susannah's first innovations: a full-day trip into Mombasa. They were visiting a mosque, the market and the fort, followed by time for shopping and lunch and then the afternoon was to be spent at the nearby sea-life park. Susannah had done all the research and preparation for the trip, visiting each stopping place to introduce herself and the hotel and to make all the arrangements. At one of her regular staff meetings, she'd discovered that Peter had an uncle who was an experienced city guide. Ten minutes in his company had convinced her that she'd found a real character who, she was sure, would appeal to the guests.

Susannah had seen another group off this morning too, on a four-day safari to the Masai Mara game park. In the future she hoped to run these trips herself, tailor-made for her guests and their particular interests. To that end, she was off the following day on a three-day trip to visit some of the safari camps. Even the fact that she was being accompanied by Clive Channing hadn't dampened her enthusiasm. Over the past three weeks, she'd come to appreciate his company. He hadn't been as attentive as she had first feared and they had fallen into a comfortable friendship, sharing the occasional coffee break and post-dinner drink, usually in the company of other guests. Channing had disappeared to Nairobi for a few days and Susannah had been surprised to discover that she was pleased to see him back. Not that she had any romantic inclinations in his direction. He just wasn't the sort of man she could ever see herself falling for. But he was good company and, Susannah acknowledged to herself at least, he was also a good buffer.

Ever since that dance on her first evening, Susannah had felt the need to keep Greg at a distance. Not that he had made any more unwelcome advances. Unspoken, they had come to an understanding: they just got on with their jobs. They met early each morning, a ten-minute business conference with Rosalind in attendance, and then went their separate ways. Once or twice they came across each other in the evenings as they wandered through the dining and lounge areas to speak to the guests. But just in case Greg was about to invite her for a drink, or worse still another dance, Susannah had got into the habit of joining Channing and whoever he was with. So, when the American had suggested they share a safari, Susannah had no hesitation in agreeing.

With many of the guests away from the hotel and the remaining ones lounging contentedly by the pools, she felt she could take an hour away from the office. She was still going to work but she wanted to find a quiet spot to firm up some more ideas that she wanted Greg to consider while she was away.

'Oh, Susannah, do you have time for a coffee?'

Susannah's thoughts were interrupted as she gathered her papers. She looked up as Rosalind put her head round the office door. The two women had quickly become friends over the past few weeks and Susannah had been pleased that Greg's secretary was coming out of her shell, even going so far as to reprimand her boss one morning for spilling his coffee over the office diary. Greg had initially looked most put out, particularly when he caught sight of Susannah's hastily covered grin. But he had apologised and even mopped the mess up himself.

46

'Yes, of course,' she replied. 'I'm going to disappear for an hour, but I'd love a coffee first.'

'Oh, good.' Rosalind smiled approvingly. 'It's about time you relaxed a bit.'

Susannah decided not to confess that she was actually going to do some planning work: her papers were in what everyone at the hotel used - a colourful beach bag - so it looked as though she really was going to relax for a change. They wandered over to the patio bar from where they could look out onto the Indian Ocean, a view that Susannah never tired of. She could still remember how startled she had been on first seeing the Indian Ocean: the brilliant turquoise of the sea had come as a complete surprise, nothing like the dark blues of the lakes back home and the complete opposite to the grey-blue of the sea off the south coast of England.

The two young women found a secluded table and immediately Peter rushed to serve them, his two favourite ladies, he called them. Soon they were chatting away. Susannah enjoyed the younger woman's company. Rosalie was extremely bright and was determined to make a career in the hotel business. Susannah sensed that Greg might have been just the slightest off-hand when hearing of his secretary's ambitions. But Susannah had encouraged the Kenyan woman and she was talking now about taking business classes in Mombasa.

'I'll talk to Greg about it, if you like,' Susannah offered, knowing that he still reduced Rosalie to a quivering silence on occasions. She had admonished him herself a couple of times and she thought that just, perhaps, he was improving in his general demeanour. Striding through reception with a face like thunder was not the best advertisement for the hotel's management, she had told him.

'I see we have a party of single ladies next week,' Susannah said to Rosalind. 'I'd like to arrange something special for them. But I'm not sure what. Perhaps they'll all make a bee-line for Greg.' She laughed at her own weak attempt at a joke.

'Well, they'll be wasting their time, then.'

'What?' Susannah was amazed at Rosalie's remark.

'He's not interested.'

'Really?' Susannah wasn't sure that she should be discussing their boss like this. But this side of Greg she had yet to see.

'Yes, really. We've had a few attractive single women here this season and, as you say, they've made a bee-line for him.'

'And?'

'Nothing.'

'Nothing?' Rosalie laughed at Susannah's disbelieving expression. 'Nothing, I promise you. He's just not interested. He's polite enough and he can put on the charm when he wants to.'

Susannah grimaced. 'He certainly can.'

'Wow, that was said with feeling!'

Susannah felt herself blush. She really must stop making such personal comments about Greg. It wouldn't do for the staff to have even an inkling of their former relationship. She tried to laugh it off.

'Oh, you know what he's like: the perfect hotel manager to the guests but a devil behind the scenes.'

Even as the words left her mouth Susannah realised she'd probably revealed too much. But, much to her relief, Rosalie joined in her laughter.

'How right you are. But he's never made a move on a guest and he's had plenty of opportunity. Even Eshe. She was really disappointed.'

Susannah sat up sharply. Rosalie had just mentioned Kenya's top international model, now making her name among the fashion houses of Paris, New York and London.

'Eshe was here?'

48

'Yes, a month or so ago, not long after Greg arrived. Her manager made the booking, saying she needed rest and privacy. But she soon made it clear she wanted Greg. Never left him alone.'

'Really?'

'Yes, she couldn't have been more obvious. But Greg didn't play along. Polite, charming, escorted her to the restaurant, bought her drinks, but that was it. Wouldn't dance with her, certainly wouldn't eat with her. I heard him explaining once, that it was company policy that staff couldn't fraternise with guests. She was furious. I doubt the Fairchild chain will ever see her again.'

'Doesn't sound at all like Greg,' Susannah's thoughts were uttered aloud before she'd had a chance to think.

'No, and you've realised that after just a few weeks.'

The guilty expression on Susannah's face must have said it all because Rosalie suddenly sat up with a quizzical and then a knowing look. 'You knew him before!'

Susannah hesitated but she realised she couldn't hold back from the woman who had become a friend.

'Yes,' she said slowly. 'I did. But it was a long time ago. We trained together, went out a couple of times, nothing serious, just a bit of fun. So I know what you're talking about.' She hoped she'd hit a light enough tone to fool Rosalie while she tried to fathom her own feelings, feelings she'd thought had long ago disappeared.

'I wondered why you two were so … so…' Rosalie searched for the right word. 'Antagonistic.'

As Susannah looked up at her friend's loud response, she saw the subject of their conversation approaching. Flustered, she waved her hand to warn Rosalie, but her friend took the gesture as a denial.

'Oh, yes, you are. Totally antagonistic. You two can barely be in the same room for five minutes before arguing,' she declared, a tad too loudly for Susannah's liking.

'Yes, but never mind that.' Susannah was recovering. 'Let's discuss that idea for next week.'

She ignored the look of total incomprehension on Rosalie's face. Greg was getting nearer.

'The single ladies. I'm sure they'd love a fashion show. What a great idea!'

'What's a great idea?'

'Oh, Mr Fairchild!' Rosalie almost jumped out of her chair, knocking the table and upsetting the remains of her coffee onto her lap. 'Oh!'

'Here, let me help.' Greg snatched up a napkin and dabbed ineffectually at the stain spreading on her skirt. The new Greg, Susannah thought. But then he spoiled the moment by adding, 'Anyone can spill a cup of coffee, can't they?'

Rosalie couldn't get up quickly enough. 'Oh, Mr Fairchild, it's all right, really. I'll go and change. I'll only be five minutes and I'll be back in the office.' With an apologetic glance at Susannah, she scrambled out of her chair and hurriedly left the bar.

Chapter 10

'So what's the great idea?' Greg queried as he took Rosalie's seat opposite Susannah.

'A fashion show, for the party of ladies coming next week.'

'Oh, god. Women!' Greg's response confirmed Rosalie's stories and Susannah couldn't help grinning.

'It'll keep them out of your hair,' she suggested.

Greg gave her a long look. 'I trust you'll be back from your little jaunt by the time they arrive?'

Susannah didn't trust herself to answer him. Little jaunt indeed! She got up from her chair and picked up her beach bag.

'Sunbathing on company time?' Greg seemed determined to get a reaction from her. A denial was once more on her lips but this time she decided to turn the tables. Greg Fairchild didn't own her.

'Yes,' she said, inwardly delighted to see the look of surprise on his face. 'Yes, I'm taking a break. My 'little jaunt' as you put it will actually be hard work: mapping the routes, choosing the best rangers, finding the most suitable times for spotting the game, making sure the meals are up to our standard ...' Susannah stopped as Greg caught hold of her wrist.

'But it won't be all work, will it?' He stood up quickly, trapping her against the table. His nearness was disconcerting.

'Yes, it will.'

'Oh, really? And what will Clive be doing? Acting as your assistant?' His grip tightened as Susannah tried to pull away. As she caught her breath to answer him back, they both heard the sound of approaching footsteps.

Greg suddenly let go of her arm and turned away.

'Oh, Mr Fairchild, there's a phone call for you, from head office. They said it was urgent.'

Peter's voice broke into Susannah's confused thoughts. Why should Greg be so concerned that Channing was going on safari with her? Could he possibly be jealous? As soon as the thought entered her head, she dismissed it. No, not Greg Fairchild. He was much more likely to be adding up the cost of the trip, of her time away from the hotel, never mind the future benefits.

'We'll talk about that matter later,' Greg threw the words over his shoulder as he strode back towards the office, leaving Susannah leaning unsteadily against the table. Trying to regain her composure, she smiled at Peter, bent to retrieve her bag and walked off in the opposite direction towards the beach.

Still thinking of Greg, Susannah wasn't taking any notice of her surroundings until she found herself on the edge of the hotel grounds, where the cultivated, if somewhat overgrown, flower beds met the woodland that fringed the beach. She started to turn back but then decided that a complete break from her working environment might be an attractive proposition. She glanced around and spotted a palm that would do nicely as a back rest. Spreading her straw mat on the ground, she sat down, made herself comfortable and got out her work file.

A variety of evening entertainment was her next priority. The band that had accompanied her and Greg on that embarrassing first night encounter would have to stay for the moment. They were adequate, she had decided, having been told by Rosalind that there was no chance of getting another band this late in the season. She would just have to come up with other ideas so that the band didn't have to play all night.

But thinking about that dance with Greg brought back memories that Susannah thought she had successfully banished. Clearly not so. The memory that came forcefully to mind was of Greg, and the last time she had seen him before finding him installed as the manager of the Sunset Beach Hotel.

The training course was coming to an end. Four of the original group had left earlier, not having made the required grade. But the rest had completed the course and had been let loose on planning an 'end of term' celebration. This could be the last time they would all see each other as the following morning they would be told where they were being sent to start work in the Fairchild empire, anywhere from London to Sydney; Los Angeles to Bombay. They might not see each other for months, if ever again.

Susannah and Greg had been growing closer. She had even begun to fantasise about him becoming a more permanent part of her life, meeting her father perhaps, even running their own game park in the future. Susannah had had boyfriends before, sons of neighbours and fellow students at university. But Greg was in a different league, and it hadn't been long before goodnight kisses on the cheek had progressed to longer, more intimate embraces. That Greg wanted more, Susannah had no doubts. Robyn Jackman had made a couple of vulgar remarks on that front to Susannah which she had ignored. But for the time being, Greg was being a gentleman, albeit with deep, tingling, lingering kisses and exciting, exploring hands.

He had asked if she would spend the weekend with him before they each went off to their new jobs and, after making him wait a day for her answer, had told him she would. The look in his eyes was enough to convince her that he was as serious about their relationship as she was, and she couldn't help but smile her way through the last days of the course.

Susannah was putting the finishing touches to the table decorations in the private room the trainees had arranged for the party. She picked up the place name cards and started arranging them, knowing that she and Greg weren't the only trainees who had begun to pair up during the course. So intent was she on getting the seating right that she didn't realise that someone had come into the room until a pair of hands grabbed her around the waist.

'What?' Susannah jumped and screamed with fright. It certainly wasn't Greg: she was too used to the smell of his after-shave now and this was definitely not his.

'Hey, jumpy tonight, aren't we?'

'Jamie. What do you think you're doing? Take your hands off me!' Susannah spun round and pushed against Jamie Dixon's chest. She knew immediately that he had started the celebrations early: she could smell beer on his breath.

'Oh, come on, Susannah. I just want a good-bye kiss. Not too much to ask for is it? I think you should share them around, after all.'

The grasp on her waist tightened as he leaned forward to put his words into action. Susannah realised two things immediately: one, that she wouldn't be able to reason with him in this state and two, that at nearly 6 feet tall and well-built, he definitely had the physical advantage. She could think of only one solution. Her right hand came up and smacked him across the cheek. He fell away from her, upending a chair and scattering cutlery, cards and wine glasses across the table.

'Why, you little bitch!'

Sensing that he was in no state for a reasoned conversation, Susannah made a dash for the door. Despite his inebriated condition, Jamie got there first, turned the key in the lock and pocketed it. Susannah looked around for another way out. But this was a small room off the main restaurant, with no windows.

'Now, Jamie, look. I'm sorry I hit you, but you surprised me and I don't like being manhandled.' Susannah was trying to calm the situation down, just as they had been

54

taught only days previously. 'Let's just say it was a misunderstanding and we can both go and get ready for this evening.'

'Oh, yes. You've got to get all dolled up for the man you don't mind manhandling you.'

'Jamie, stop it. That's nothing to do with you.' Susannah was devastated that that was how Jamie and, no doubt, the rest of the trainees saw her.

'But he isn't who he says he is. Did you know that?' Jamie was advancing on her again and Susannah had to back away, stepping over the shattered glasses and crushed flowers.

'What do you mean?'

'Oh, so he hasn't told you? The great Greg Chambers, or should I say Greg Fairchild?' Jamie shouted the last word in her face as she stopped in her retreat.

'What?'

'Oh, yes. He's been undercover. Probably daddy's spy, to see what we all get up to. He's a jetsetter, Susannah dear. Girlfriends all over the globe. Not surprising with the fortune he's going to inherit.'

'I don't believe you.'

The words came out of her mouth, but Susannah's mind was working overtime. It fitted, of course it did. He was smart, smarter than all the other men on the course; he was confident, suave, glib, and look at his car - hardly bought on the means of a mere trainee. What could he have seen in her? Jamie's next words answered her unspoken question.

'He's been trifling with you, Susannah. A mere diversion while on the course. He'll be moving on to starlets in Hollywood, models in Paris and ladies at Ascot. He won't want some mousy female hanging around. A parasite, that was it,' Jamie was warming to his theme. 'That's what he called you, my dear. Someone who leans on everyone else. He's going places and not with you. Your father's two-bit place is hardly in the same league, is it? You don't know anything about this business, that's what he said. He's been helping you out, for his own amusement. Doubts that you'll ever stand on your own feet.' He laughed at his own words but his laughter was cut short as they both heard loud banging on the door.

'Susannah, are you there? Susannah?'

'Yes, I am. We're just having trouble with the lock.' Susannah glared at Jamie, knowing that he could hardly contradict her when it was their course leader calling.

Jamie pushed roughly past her and unlocked the door. Never one to lose an opportunity, he added, 'There we are, Susannah. Just needs a man's touch.'

Susannah ignored him as he slipped away. 'Did you want me?'

'Yes, Susannah, there's phone call for you. From Harare. Take it in the office.'

Half an hour later, Susannah remembered, she had left the hotel. Her father had been attacked by poachers and was in hospital. She had packed quickly while the course leader organised a taxi and a plane ticket. Only as she walked out of the hotel for the last time did she spare Greg a thought. Was it true that he was a Fairchild? A burst of laughter made her look back and there he was. When he saw her, his expression darkened and he said something to the man at his side, Jamie Dixon. She couldn't hear their muttered exchange, but she could read his eyes. They said he wanted nothing more to do with her.

The unpleasant memory brought Susannah sharply back to the present and she chided herself for wasting time. That was all in the past. Now they knew exactly where they stood: as work colleagues. For one more moment Susannah allowed herself to wonder what Greg had been doing in the intervening years, while she had been nursing her father. Why had he ended up in such an obviously run-down hotel like the

Sunset Beach? As heir to the Fairchild fortune, surely he could have had the pick of their empire? Why bother with the Sunset Beach at all? The Fairchild Corporation could easily have offloaded it to a smaller chain or a local enterprise. So why was the great Greg Fairchild here, in the back of beyond?

A sudden noise in the trees behind her shook Susannah wide awake. She realised with a shock that she must have fallen asleep, and she had needed this hour to work on her plans. Damn. But as she hastily looked through her notes, she was pleased to see that they only needed a few minutes' work to make them presentable. More evening entertainments, more day trips and a couple of themed parties; she had been jotting down ideas whenever she thought of them and she was optimistic that Greg would be receptive to at least some of them.

Soon after the cocktail party on her first evening, she had tried to find out what the bar receipts had been. Greg had not been pleased at the free drinks that she and Channing had been handing out – in fact, wildly angry would actually be more exact – but she was hoping that the guests' spending at the party afterwards had almost made up for it. She had learned from Peter that Greg had taken the receipts that same evening.

'Trust him to be quick off the mark when money's involved,' she had thought. At her crestfallen expression, Peter had told her not to worry, he was sure they hadn't taken anything like that in one evening ever since he'd been there and that was in three years.

Even so, Susannah knew that Greg would mark down any loss in profits as her fault and it would probably take a lot more than the occasional coach trip to get the hotel turned around.

The noise in the trees was getting louder and Susannah was aware that people were coming in her direction.

She gathered her papers, ready to leave. But then a voice stopped her.

'I'd be careful if I were you.' The voice was Greg's and he wasn't warning his companion of an overhanging branch. He sounded much too determined.

'What d'you mean?' There was no mistaking Clive's voice either.

Before Susannah could move, Greg made it clear what he was warning Channing about.

'She's out for what she can get. I nearly fell for it once. But never again.'

It wasn't so much the words that brought a sickening feeling to Susannah's stomach; it was much more the tone in which they had been delivered: bitterness, anger and sheer hostility. He was talking about her!

'Hey, whatever's gone on between the two of you, that's all in the past, Greg.' Channing sounded not a little put out at the other man's outburst. 'People change, you know. I've got to know her pretty well over the last few weeks and she doesn't come across like that at all.'

'Well, it only took me a few weeks to find out what she's really like and take it from me, I had a lucky escape.'

Susannah couldn't believe what she was hearing. If anyone had had a lucky escape five years ago, it had been her. Escape from a scalp-hunting, lying, two-faced, womanising impostor.

'A gold-digger, Clive, that's what she is. All she wants is a rich husband. I reckon you're her next target!'

Chapter 11

'She's good, isn't she?'

Greg glanced over at his companion who had just broken the silence of the early evening.

'Have you read these?' Channing gestured towards the file of papers that Susannah had given Greg when their paths had crossed in the office that afternoon.

'No,' Greg knew his response was brief, curt even, but he had no other words. Clive had interrupted his thoughts and, inevitably, those thoughts had been about Susannah. So his comments about her being good had been a bit too near the mark.

'You should and soon. I think all these ideas will brighten the place up, even get guests from other hotels coming over of an evening.'

'Really?' Greg raised an eyebrow and tried not to sound disbelieving. He had told Susannah that he would look over her afternoon's work while she was away on her jaunt, and he hadn't given it another thought. But when he and Channing had met up for a pre-dinner drink, the American had commented how quiet the hotel was; 'too quiet', were his exact words.

'So, have a look at these,' Greg had replied and passed over Susannah's file.

'Yes, really.' Channing was insistent. 'I guess if you two have history, then it'll take a miracle for you to believe me. But I think she's on the right lines. She knows how to write a proposal – it's all there, Greg, ideas, costs, projections, contacts. A first-class job.'

'Ok, ok. You don't have to do the hard sell too.' Greg forced a smile and took the file from Channing. The older man had become something of a confidante in the past few weeks. He knew the hotel business, at least in the States, and he was on an extended holiday-cum-business trip in Africa, always on the look-out for new ventures to invest in. He hadn't forced his opinions, but Greg had realised early on that he could benefit from the American's experience.

Channing rose from the table, downing his beer. 'I'm off for dinner,' he said. 'I've promised Mildred and Homer that I'll make up a four for bridge.'

The thought of a whole evening in the company of the Armitages horrified Greg but he could see the twinkle in Channing's eyes that meant that he was going to have a fun evening. He knew that mixing with the guests wasn't his one of his strongest skills: he was a back scenes man, wheeling and dealing. Susannah was far better with people. There, he was thinking of Susannah again. Why did everything have to come back to her?

Well, she was going away for a few days, so he'd be able to get some real work done, he thought. Let Channing deal with her flirtatious ways. He had been warned, after all.

Waving a hand at Peter for another beer, Greg decided that he would give Susannah's ideas a quick glance. But fifteen minutes later he was on his second detailed read through, pen in hand, making his own notes, comments and costings in the margins. Yes, her suggestions were good, he admitted to himself. All bar one. Well, she couldn't expect him to give her carte blanche, he reasoned. Her costings and projections weren't that far off, too, although he would have to err a little more on the cautious side. But, with a bit of luck, the Sunset Beach Hotel might just be able to establish itself as an entertainment venue for this part of the coast.

It was, after all, one of the larger hotels along this stretch, most of the others being little more than guesthouses with no facilities to compare. Their nearest competitor, as Greg thought of it, was the Majestic, a drive of some fifteen miles away. He knew they were getting the cream of the tourists just now. The hotel was only a couple of years old, still very fresh and modern looking. But even they didn't have the breadth of evening attractions that Susannah was suggesting.

'Mr Fairchild? Coo-ee.' He couldn't escape the eagle eye of Mildred Armitage. The elderly couple from Miami were, like Channing, on an extended tour, returning to the Sunset Beach after various trips to the game parks, Nairobi, Malindi and even into Tanzania. 'Now, Mr Fairchild, I'm sure you'll be able to help.'

Greg put on what he thought was his perfect smile for guests, mindful of Susannah's rather cutting remark about his 'thunder face'. 'Mrs Armitage,' he began.

'Now, now, it's Mildred. I've told you that a hundred times,' she giggled. 'After all, we're no strangers after all these weeks, are we?'

'No, of course not.' Greg reluctantly closed Susannah's file and stood up, holding his breath at what Mildred had in store this time. He was soon answered.

'Bridge.'

'Bridge?'

'Yes, bridge. We need a fourth, Mr Fairchild. Just for a couple of hours after dinner. It will do you a world of good to get away from work for a while.' Mildred waved dismissively at the file on the table.

'But I thought Mr Channing was….'

Again Mildred had an instant reply. 'Oh, yes, he's playing. Wonderful man. But that nice Mrs Carberry has found herself a partner for the dancing.'

If she had been near enough, Greg was sure Mildred would have quite literally dug him in the ribs. As it was, the wink said everything about the matchmaking possibilities of the dance classes that Susannah had introduced, persuading one of the band members to act as instructor.

'Mrs … er ... Mildred, I would have loved to have joined you this evening, but I have an engagement, and yes, it is work that I cannot possibly get out of at this late stage. I'm sure you'll understand.'

'Oh.' The disappointment was acute. 'Well, I do think you work too hard. That nice Miss Susannah too. Always rushing around she is, looking after everyone, guests and staff. Don't think I haven't noticed, Mr Fairchild. I just hope she's properly appreciated?'

Greg could see a way out. 'Actually, Mildred,' he bent down and lowered his voice conspiratorially. 'That's just what I am doing tonight, giving Susannah a bit of a break. I'd rather not disappoint her …'

He didn't have to say any more. Mildred patted him on the arm and gave him an approving smile.

'Excellent, Mr Fairchild. You do just that. I don't think that girl's had an evening off since she's arrived. I don't need to tell you she's a diamond. You just have to hold on to good staff.'

'Absolutely, Mildred.' Greg made the stock reply automatically but then found himself thinking about it. Susannah was good for the hotel. Mildred Armitage was right and so was Channing. He should be able to put any personal feelings aside and concentrate on business. So that's exactly what he was going to do, starting tonight.

Chapter 12

'So I'd like to go through them with you tonight,' Greg had found Susannah in the dining-room, chatting to the staff as they prepared the tables. Mildred Armitage was right, he thought for the second time in half an hour. Susannah did work hard, and she was good with staff and guests alike.

'Tonight?'

'Yes, tonight. I don't think either of us will be needed here – the dance lessons are arranged, as are the bridge tables.'

Her expression told him that she was surprised he knew what was going on.

'So, I thought we'd go and spy on the competition,' Greg was enjoying Susannah's evident bewilderment. 'Dinner. At the Majestic. I'll see you in the foyer at eight.'

He gave her no opportunity to question his arrangements and turned away, realising with a shock that he was actually looking forward to her company for a few hours, away from their working environment.

'What are you smiling at?' Greg glanced at Susannah as they pulled away from the hotel. He had turned down the offer of a driver when he had gone round to the garages and had selected the least dilapidated of the hotel's meagre selection of vehicles: an open-top jeep that had definitely seen better days.

Susannah seemed a little embarrassed. 'Oh, just the car,' she replied, and he immediately caught her drift: the last time he had taken her out for a meal, it had been in his Porsche.

Assuming that neither of them wished to dwell on those days, he smiled briefly and turned his attention back to the road. 'Do you know the Majestic?'

'Only by reputation,' Susannah replied. 'Rosalie was saying she's been to a couple of wedding parties there.'

'There's another idea,' Greg interrupted.

'What?' Susannah sounded flustered and Greg put it down to a particularly sharp turn he'd made on the rutted mud road. He made a conscious effort to slow down; Susannah had never been impressed by his fast driving in the Porsche.

'Wedding parties,' he repeated. 'Hopefully that's something we might attract in the future.'

'Oh, yes, right,' Susannah said. 'It's becoming quite the thing, I believe, getting married in the tropics.'

There was an uneasy silence as Greg negotiated more tricky turns. He began to think he'd made a mistake in taking Susannah away from the Sunset Beach. Would it be like this all evening? Each of them overly careful about what to say, their past hanging unspoken in the air?

'So, Mildred and Homer …'

'Rosalie's really keen …'

They both spoke at once and broke off simultaneously.

'After you,' Greg's new-found courtesy was lost as Susannah's words echoed his. They both laughed, nervously, and silence descended on the car once again.

'You were saying about Rosalie.' Greg was determined to be positive. He didn't want to antagonise Susannah at the start of their evening out. 'She's spoken to me about the course. Now that I've seen the details and the college brochure, I'm a lot happier about it. I think you're right, it would do her good to learn some computer skills.'

This time Susannah laughed naturally, surprising Greg. At first he thought she was making fun of what had almost been an apology from him. But as she turned towards him, he could see the old sparkle in her eyes.

'Perhaps she's not the only one who needs a computer course?' she suggested with a smile.

Greg's mind went blank for a moment and then he realised what she was referring to. On the Fairchild training course, the one thing he hadn't particularly excelled in was computer skills. He was competent enough: Greg Fairchild would never admit defeat in anything. But a couple of times Susannah had come to his rescue when the blessed thing had seemingly eaten all his work.

He returned her smile. 'Ok,' he said. 'Not one of my strengths, I'll admit it. All the more reason for Rosalie to get qualified.'

Susannah nodded in agreement and the rest of their journey was spent in discussing Rosalie, Peter and other members of staff. By the time they reached their destination, Greg felt more relaxed and thought that Susannah was too. Perhaps this hadn't been such a bad idea.

'Wow!' Susannah's appreciative gasp was spontaneous as they were shown into the Tamarind Bistro, the smaller and more exclusive of the Majestic's two restaurants. Certainly it outshone anything the Sunset Beach could offer. There were only eight tables, separated by low trellis dividers which were covered in flowers. The rest of the décor was tropical too: brightly painted jungle and animal scenes on the walls, the occasional palm tree, low green lights and background music of a distinctive Caribbean flavour.

One side of the bistro opened out onto a small patio area which was screened off from the rest of the hotel grounds. The overall effect was one of luxurious exclusivity, particularly as there were only two other couples in the restaurant. Greg and Susannah were shown to a table by the patio, the waiter attentively holding Susannah's chair before Greg could claim that privilege.

'So, what do you think? Nice, isn't it?' Greg was impressed with how quickly the waiter had taken their order and had served their first course: lobster bisque for him while Susannah had chosen seafood cocktail. He was expecting her to rave about their surroundings. But after her initial comment as they had entered, she had become quiet.

'It certainly gives a good impression,' she said slowly.

'But?'

Susannah didn't answer straight away. Instead, she put down her fork, neatly wiped her lips and gave him her full attention. 'Greg, are you really interested in what I think? Or would I be wasting my time, like all that work I did on my ideas for the Sunset Beach? You haven't mentioned those yet. I need to know.'

Greg was taken aback by her intensity. This, for Susannah, was clearly no relaxing evening out. She fully expected to be talking shop and she clearly expected her opinions to count. Suddenly, he realised that her opinions would count and that they did, indeed, matter to him. She was staring at him, waiting for his reply. But at that moment, the attentive waiter returned to clear their plates.

'I hope you enjoyed that, sir, madam,' he said. Greg nodded and expected Susannah to do the same.

'Just a little too much salt in the mayonnaise,' she said quietly. 'But otherwise, good.'

The waiter looked momentarily startled but recovered quickly and left.

'Well, I'd expect the Sunset Beach guests to say if a dish wasn't to their liking. How else are we going to find out what's right and what's not?' Susannah's voice had risen as she had gone on the defensive at Greg's look of surprise.

'I couldn't agree more,' Greg said. Gently he put his hand on top of hers. 'But I rather wanted to stay incognito tonight.'

Susannah withdrew her hand quickly and apologised. 'Yes, yes, of course. Sorry.'

'No apology needed, Susannah. I just thought you'd like to see what the opposition was like and get away from work for a while.'

'So you don't want to talk about my ideas, then?' Susannah kept her voice low, but the words came out just as strongly as before.

'No, yes, of course I do,' Greg wasn't sure how to respond. 'I do want to discuss your ideas. But I thought we might get away from shop-talk for a while.'

A silence greeted his remark and he could see a wariness creep into her eyes.

'Oh, Susannah.' It was his turn to be exasperated now. 'I thought things had been going well recently.' He waited for a response but carried on when it was clear that none was forthcoming. 'Let's put what happened all those years ago behind us.'

Susannah waited for what seemed like an age to Greg before she answered.

'All right. I think that's best. We have to work together, don't we? One thing they did teach us on the training course was how to keep our feelings hidden from the people who really matter.'

Greg knew there was a sub-text to Susannah's words. But considering it had been she who had been in the wrong back then, he was amazed at her effrontery in reminding him how to behave. He was about to make a sharp retort but once again the waiter interrupted the moment. By the time their main courses had been served, he had cooled down, a feeling that surprised him.

'Ok,' he forced his voice to sound bright and friendly with no hint of past feelings. 'I think your ideas are excellent. I'd like you to start work on most of them as soon as you get back from your …' he paused. The word jaunt was on his lips. But in this new spirit of cooperation, he felt he had to at least compromise. Him. Greg Fairchild. Compromising for a woman! So his next words came out with something like a sigh. 'When you're back from your planning trip,' he finished.

He half-expected Susannah to comment on his choice of words. If she did, then he didn't think he could sustain this new Greg Fairchild. But she too sounded as though she was making an effort.

'Thank you, Greg. That means a lot. Which did you want me to start with?'

The next hour passed quickly as they discussed Susannah's ideas in detail. Greg was impressed by the way she responded positively to his few countersuggestions, usually for financial reasons. Greg remembered that Susannah had put her name on the list to run a couple of safari slide evenings: entertainment for those who just wanted a beach holiday, but also a great advertisement for their own safaris that she was about to organise.

'Where did you take all your slides?' he asked. The conversation had been flowing well, with friendly bantering and not a few laughs. So Greg was surprised when Susannah fell silent at his question.

'Oh, mostly in my father's game park,' she replied quietly, picking up the menu and studying it intently.

It was on the tip of Greg's tongue to ask how her father was. Unbidden, his thoughts went back to that last day on the training course and Susannah's hurried departure. The other trainees had been told that her father had been in an accident. At the time, he had dismissed the idea, thinking it a good excuse so she could avoid him, having been unmasked as a gold-digger. But he realised that it would bring those memories back for her too and they had been successful in putting that behind them. The new Greg decided that he would try to show a caring side.

Susannah was holding the menu up, hiding her face, so he put out a hand and gently pulled it down only to be shocked to see tears in her eyes. 'Susannah?'

'Excuse me,' Susannah rose from the table. 'I have something in my eye. I won't be long. Would you order the fruit salad for me, please?'

Greg rose too but Susannah quickly pushed her chair back and rushed to the cloakroom. When she returned, she appeared to be totally composed once more. Greg decided it would be best not to refer to her slide shows – that was clearly what had upset her – but started talking about another of her ideas.

'A visit to the local craft factory,' he said. 'I like it.'

'Good,' Susannah responded brightly. 'I went down there yesterday, Rosalie came with me.'

'On her day off?'

'Yes, Greg, on her day off.'

'Ok, ok, carry on,' Greg waved his spoon as apology for interrupting her, but he was impressed.

'Anyway, we found that the locals produce some really excellent crafts, not the usual tourist stuff you get in town.'

'You mean with Welcome to Mombasa written on everything?'

'Exactly.' They laughed companionably. Susannah described what they had seen and how she had spoken to the manager. He'd been delighted at her idea of bringing small groups of visitors to the factory, even suggesting that he would select one or two of his workers to talk to them.

'I just hope he doesn't put his prices up,' Greg couldn't keep the businessman down for long.

'Actually, Greg, I made that point,' Susannah said. 'Although I think I was a little more subtle.'

They smiled at each other and conversation stopped for a few moments. Their eyes held each other's, Greg thinking how lovely she looked. She used only the tiniest amount of make-up – he remembered that from before – not needing any artificial enhancement of her features. He opened his mouth to speak, not sure what was going to come out.

But at that precise moment, the band started playing on the far side of the patio. Another of the couples wasted no time in getting up to dance and, in perfect keeping with the ambiance of the moment, Greg rose too. He held out his hand and there was just the merest hint of hesitation before Susannah put down her napkin and rose from the table, putting her hand in his. Greg led her onto the small dance floor, moving his hand to her waist. Again, a momentary hesitation, or was he imagining it? But then Susannah put her hand on his shoulder, and he clasped her other hand in his.

All the old feelings came back. Dancing with her had always been good, whether it had been in the compulsory dance lessons on the training course or in the more intimate restaurants he had taken her to in the Kent countryside. They danced well together: any observer might have thought they had been together for years so well-matched were they. In time honoured fashion, two quicksteps were followed by two waltzes and then the band changed the pace with one of those indeterminate pieces where some couples persist in ballroom dancing while others simply slow down to an intimate swaying to the beat. Greg held Susannah closer, resting his cheek lightly against hers. He let go of her hand and held her waist, forcing her to put both her hands on his shoulders. Greg lost himself in the music and the scent of Susannah's hair and her skin.

When the band slid into another tune, he leaned back slightly to look at her. Disappointingly, he detected wariness in her eyes. 'It's your evening off,' he whispered, not expecting a reply.

'I thought we were spying,' came the retort, tinged with suppressed laughter.

The old Greg would have taken umbrage at what was clearly not the same romantic, sensual experience for his companion. But the new Greg joined in Susannah's clearly lighter mood. 'But we might as well enjoy ourselves as we spy.'

They finished the dance in a comfortable silence and Greg led her off the dance floor and back to their table where coffee awaited them. He didn't want to spoil the mood, nor did he want to carry on talking shop. But it was Susannah who started the conversation again, making it clear that the dancing had been an interlude, and that she was here to work.

'So, I'll go ahead, shall I, with the factory visits, the fashion show for next month, the slide shows after that and more of the local dancing?'

'Fine, yes,' Greg tried really hard not to let his annoyance show. But it wasn't Susannah he was annoyed with; it was himself. She was talking business, and he didn't want to! That was the effect she was having on him. Perhaps it was just as well she was going away for a few days.

The drive home was quiet. Greg was concentrating on the road but was also occupied with his own thoughts. He thought Susannah might be too but then noticed she was finding it difficult to stay awake. As they pulled into the driveway of the Sunset Beach, she sat up, rubbing her eyes.

'So sorry. Did I drop off?' She turned to smile at him, her sleepy expression making his heart beat faster. She looked so lovely, so vulnerable. He leaned closer, but unlike on the dance floor, this time she moved away.

'Susannah, wait!' There was an urgency in Greg's voice and Susannah responded by turning round to face him, her hand on the handle of the car door.

'Yes?' She was clearly wide awake now and any romantic notions Greg might have been entertaining were quickly dashed.

'I just wanted to say thank you for a most pleasant evening,' he paused, expecting her to respond likewise.

'Thank you, Greg. It was good to get away from the hotel for a while. A refreshing change.' Refreshing? He could feel his blood beginning to boil. 'It was great to be able to sort out all those ideas. Now, we're on the right track, I'm sure of it.'

Greg could hardly disagree with her. 'Yes, yes, that's true. It was a good opportunity. But there's one other thing I wanted to say.'

Susannah looked at him, a half-smile on her lips. Maybe the evening's mood wasn't yet over. 'Yes?'

Rarely had Greg felt so out of his depth. He realised he had lost the initiative tonight. He'd best give in gracefully so that he'd have another opportunity when she returned from her trip. 'Just that I think your tailor-made safaris are a great idea, another great idea,' he smiled at her. 'Don't take any notice of what I said before. You deserve a break, you've been working hard and I'm not sure you've had a day off since you've arrived.'

Silently he thanked Mildred Armitage for her observation. 'Have a good time. I think you'll find Channing will be good company.'

For a second, he thought Susannah looked startled. His complete about-face must certainly have come as something of a shock, plus his goodwill towards her and the American. But he just wasn't prepared for her parting words as she flung the car door open. Her voice had a distinctly sarcastic edge.

'Why, thank you, Greg. It's so nice to have the boss's approval of my travelling companion. But aren't you worried for him? After all, he'll be all alone for three days with a husband-hunting gold-digger!'

Chapter 13

'Well, isn't this just the most perfect day?' Clive Channing the Third was clearly in expansive mood. For once, Susannah felt completely in harmony with him. It was only six o'clock in the morning, but she too felt in that sort of humour: happy to be alive and in anticipation of a good trip away.

'It certainly is, couldn't be better,' Susannah replied with a big smile, just as Clive came up and enveloped her in a friendly hug. As they broke apart laughing, Susannah caught the slightest of movements behind her, in the hotel foyer. But when she turned to look properly, she could see nothing. It was too early for the breakfast staff and none of their present guests were particularly early risers. A thought crossed her mind, but she dismissed it immediately. Even if it had been Greg, he could hardly have cause for complaint when he had told her quite clearly that Channing would be a good companion.

As they loaded their bags into the jeep, Susannah realised that her good mood had a lot to do with the fact that she had had one of the best night's sleep since arriving at the Sunset Beach. That, she believed, was because of her parting words to Greg the previous evening. How she had had the nerve, she didn't know. Five years ago she'd never have spoken to anyone, let alone him, like that. But now she felt that they each knew where they stood, personally and professionally, and she felt a whole lot happier as a result.

'Is this your whole wardrobe?' Clive's teasing words broke into Susannah's thoughts. Their driver was bringing out more bags and carefully packing them into the back of the vehicle.

'Now, Clive, I did warn you that this was going to be a working trip for me,' Susannah started to explain.

'Yes, but I didn't think we'd be wining and dining for a month!' Clive joked as he took hold of a particularly heavy bag.

'That's my computer,' Susannah warned, although her companion was being extremely careful as he stowed it. 'I have my camera equipment too.'

'Hey, you know me, just teasing,' he replied. 'You've got some serious technology here.'

'It's a serious business, game shooting,' she replied.

His head jerked up suddenly from the depths of the jeep and for a moment he looked concerned. 'Shooting?'

'Cameras, shooting?' Susannah smiled at his misunderstanding.

'Oh, yes, of course. Silly me.'

'But I know what you mean,' she continued as they both got in and settled themselves in the back of the jeep. 'There are still people who come out here expecting to go on a game shoot. They just don't realise that it's all carefully controlled nowadays. If it wasn't, we soon wouldn't have many of these animals left.'

Clive nodded in agreement and the two of them were soon in deep discussion about the future of Kenya's wildlife. Their driver, Mohammed, joined in the conversation at Susannah's prompting: he had been chosen specially for this trip because of his knowledge of the Masai Mara game reserve where they were headed, and Susannah was keen to hear his opinions.

After a while she realised that Clive had gone quiet. 'Sorry,' she apologised. 'Are we boring you?'

'Not in the slightest, my dear,' Clive replied. 'I'm just more than happy listening to you both. It's great to hear two people so into their subject. You know, Susi,' he paused and lowered his voice. 'I don't think Greg appreciates what an expert he has in you.'

'Oh, Clive.' Susannah felt just the slightest bit embarrassed at Channing's remark; they shouldn't really be discussing her boss like this. 'I'm sure he does.'

'Well, I shall certainly make sure he knows when we get back,' Clive declared. 'I think you could make the Sunset Beach into quite an attraction for wildlife enthusiasts, the more serious ones as well as the tourists. That should be your speciality, Susi. Get this off the ground and I reckon you're onto a winner.'

'Thank you, Clive.' Susannah was a bit overwhelmed at the businessman's confidence in her. A nice change, she thought. She gave herself a mental shake and promised herself, I'll show them both. Clive smiled at her, and she realised that her emotions must be showing. She grinned back at him. This was going to be a most enjoyable trip – and with something to show Greg Fairchild at the end.

'I'm going to insist, Susi.' Clive was clearly not going to take 'no' for an answer and after a most fascinating but tiring day Susannah was content to let him take the lead. They had arrived an hour ago at the Lodge and both had been impressed with the high standard of accommodation offered out here in the bush. Clive had suggested that they freshen up and then meet for dinner; work, for the day, was finished.

When Susannah had been shown to her room, she couldn't help but compare her luxurious surroundings with those she and her father had offered at their camp back in what had then been Rhodesia, now Zimbabwe. Her parents, after ten years of marriage and a home in Bulawayo, had decided to leave city life behind and had taken over an old farmhouse on the edge of the bush. They had slowly developed it into a respectable business: organising safari trips for small parties. Over the years they had added a few rooms, employed one or two kitchen staff as and when trade demanded, but basically had kept it simple and homely.

Susannah, born there, had grown up with an innate love of the countryside and animals. It had been a perfectly natural progression for her to study zoology at the country's top university with the aim of returning to the family business.

But how often did things turn out as one expected? Susannah mused as she washed off the dust of the day under a wonderfully refreshing shower. Her mother had died while she was at university and although her father had carried on, encouraging her to finish the course, the spark had gone from his life. On her trips home, Susannah had seen how the business was failing, and she was impatient to get back and help.

But then, things had turned around. More guests started appearing, rooms were re-decorated and her father seemed much more able to cope. He persuaded his daughter to attend the Fairchild Corporation's training scheme so that she would have all the business acumen and experience at her fingertips when the time was right for her to take over the family concern. But the poachers attacking her father had brought all those plans to an end.

The following years had been spent nursing her father and when he died, Susannah had learned the truth: that her father had sold out to a local businessman and what she thought had been her home and her livelihood was nothing whatsoever to do with her.

'I'm dwelling too much on the past,' Susannah chided herself as she dressed for dinner. She had come to accept that her father had done what he thought best at the time: selling out so that she would at least have some money in the bank and not a failing business to inherit when he was gone. It just proved how naïve she had been, Susannah thought. When the business had started looking up, she hadn't questioned where the money to re-decorate had come from. Nor had she questioned what they were living on when she returned home to nurse her father.

But now she was much more aware of the finances behind a successful business. Gosh, she was almost sounding like Greg! She laughed out loud at the thought as she checked her appearance in the mirror. She had known that the safari lodges out here were smart places. True, a lot of their visitors came in large coach parties from the big hotels in Nairobi and Mombasa and they would think nothing of dining in the same clothes they had been travelling in all day. But, like the Majestic, some of the lodges had a luxury side: private areas for exclusive parties where something of a past age of elegant dining was still observed.

Accordingly, she had brought a couple of her smartest evening dresses with her – outfits that she had never had the opportunity to wear at the Sunset Beach. Not having been brought up in the city, Susannah hadn't been one for obsessing with cosmetics and high fashion, as had many of her contemporaries at university. She wasn't particularly enamoured of the way her fellow students needed almost constant reassurance as to how they looked.

And she certainly hadn't taken to the ministrations of Robyn Jackman on the Fairchild training course. She had told Susannah in no uncertain terms that she wasn't making enough of her natural beauty. She had been so persistent that Susannah had given in one evening and had allowed Robyn to give her a make-up lesson. The results had been dramatic: just what the well-dressed young woman was wearing for city life. But Susannah had rushed back to the safety of her own room and washed everything off. Robyn hadn't bothered with her again.

But Susannah did have one thing to thank Robyn for, she realised with an ironic laugh. She had been scathing of Susannah's wardrobe and in a moment of defiance, Susannah had taken herself off to London's Bond Street and bought herself an evening dress, intended for her romantic weekend with Greg at the end of their course. It had never been worn.

When she had been packing for this safari trip, Susannah had decided that now was the right time to put those memories behind her. She'd been relieved when she had tried the dress on, and it had still fitted. Susannah had lost weight following her father's death but had clearly put it back once she had settled in at the Sunset Beach, enjoying the hotel's international cuisine and the occasional calorie-laden pastry with Rosalind during their coffee breaks.

Susannah had spotted the dress immediately, despite the efforts of the insistent sales girl to divert her towards more trendy outfits. It was the colour of the sunset back home on the family game reserve: vibrant reds melting into swirls of orange and pink, the silk falling in gentle drapes like the sky itself. It was perfect, she had thought at the time.

Now, as she stood in front of the mirror, she knew that the dress still suited her, even though a different man, a completely different man, would see her in it. Even so, she was somewhat embarrassed when she went downstairs to the dining room and was greeted with a loud wolf-whistle by Channing, dressed to the nines in his tuxedo. 'Wow, Susi, you look stunning.'

She decided to play him at his own game. 'So do you, Clive. What a pair we make!'

They laughed companionably and it set the tone for the rest of the evening.

Chapter 14

The staff at the lodge had explained to them on their arrival that the manager was due back from leave the following day when he'd be delighted to talk to them about their plans for the Sunset Beach guests. So tonight, it was just the two of them, the other guests having already eaten in preparation for an early start the following day.

'This sure is a lovely place, Susi,' Clive said, looking around in admiration. Wherever possible, there were large picture windows providing the most magnificent views of the surrounding bush. From the dining room, Susannah and Clive could see a floodlit watering-hole which, they had been told, would attract a variety of wildlife later in the evening.

'Have you been to others like this?'

'No, I haven't,' Susannah admitted and for perhaps the first time since her change of circumstances, she felt perfectly at ease when she added, 'Our safari camp wasn't anywhere near as luxurious.'

'Your safari camp?' Clive queried.

'Yes, my parents had a much smaller business in Rhodesia, 50 kilometres from Bulawayo.'

Clive stopped eating and looked at Susannah. 'I never knew that,' he said. 'Tell me about it.'

Maybe because she had been thinking over old times earlier and because they had been getting on so well all day, Susannah was quite content to tell Clive about her family and their life in the Rhodesian bush. He really seemed interested, and Susannah became relaxed enough to recount some of the amusing incidents that had occurred over the years.

On finishing their meal, they were invited to move to a comfortable seating area by the window for their coffee and Clive encouraged Susannah to continue with her story. It was only when she reached the part about her father's accident, that she paused, stumbled and then just stopped.

'That must have been a terrible time for you, Susi,' Clive said gently, touching her briefly on the shoulder. 'It was,' she replied quietly. 'I was on a training course and I had to leave. I was supposed to work for the company for at least a year after the course. But of course I couldn't. I stayed with my father, and we coped as best we could. He died earlier this year.'

'Oh, my dear.' Clive moved closer to Susannah's side and put an arm round her shoulders. For a second or two, Susannah kept it together. But Clive's obvious compassion was almost too much too bear and she was unable to stop the tears.

'Hey, it's ok. I understand. You've been through a helluva lot these past few months, haven't you?'

Susannah could only nod. She reached for her bag and found a tissue to wipe her eyes. Gradually she regained her composure. Clive indicated to the waiter that they wanted a coffee refill and, when it came, pressed Susannah to drink. She did so, grateful for the genuine concern and comfort from her companion. For a few minutes, they sat in silence, looking out of the windows at a group of honey-badgers that had appeared at the watering-hole.

'Are you all right, Susi?'

'Yes, thank you, Clive,' Susannah turned towards him, grateful for his sensitivity. 'I'm fine now. I haven't spoken to anyone much about Dad. Thank you for listening.'

Surprising herself, Susannah leant forward and gave him a kiss on his cheek.

'Hey, glad to be of assistance,' he replied, kissing her gently in return.

'Anytime you need some broad shoulders, mine are available.'

'Thank you.'

They turned back to the scene outside and for the next twenty minutes became engrossed in watching what was almost a parade of animals: water buffalo, zebra, impala and finally, a family of elephants.

'Would you like a night-cap?' Clive called the waiter over. Susannah was not a great drinker. That was one of the other things that had separated her from the other university students, who always seemed to be out on the town, drinking 'til all hours. But tonight, she thought, that was just what she needed.

'Yes, I would. Thank you. A brandy would hit the spot nicely.'

Susannah knew it was late. She really ought to get back to her room and make a few notes of what the day had brought: their route, the animals they had seen, plus, of course, her impressions of the Lodge. She wanted to have a full report written by the time they got back so that, with Greg's approval, they could start sending out their own safaris as soon as possible.

But it was good to take time out too. She hadn't really relaxed like this for months. Clive was a comfortable companion, easy to talk to and be with. They enjoyed a light-hearted flirtation. This was turning out to be just the break she had needed. Susannah suddenly realised that Clive was talking to her.

'Sorry, Clive, I was miles away,' she said, a little untruthfully.

'I didn't want to break the mood, Susi. But there was something I wanted to ask you.'

'Yes?' Susannah sat up straighter, these chairs were really too comfortable.

'You said it was your family concern, that safari camp in Rhodesia. Yes?'

She nodded in agreement.

'So what are you doing here, or rather at the Sunset Beach? Why are you working for Greg? You could do so much better on your own.'

Clive's voice had risen and Susannah was quite shocked by his intensity. 'Clive?'

Channing distractedly waved his hands in apology. He got up and wandered a little way away, clearly taking time out to calm down. Susannah had no idea what she should do. Why had he reacted like that? She thought he was a friend, or at the very least a close business contact of Greg's. So why the outburst about her doing better on her own? Perhaps Greg had put him up to it? Did he really want to get rid of her that much that he had to get her safari companion to suggest it? The idea was ridiculous. Wasn't it?

Susannah knew that Greg hadn't wanted her there in the first place. He'd made that plain enough. But she thought, she really thought they had been getting on better recently. He liked her ideas, the hotel was running more smoothly, they had reached a working relationship. Did he really still want her to go? Was it all because of last night?

Susannah's reasoning took another turn. But she still couldn't believe Greg could be so petty. She had rejected his advances. No, that was too strong a word for it. She had merely avoided what might have turned into an embarrassing goodnight kiss. Was that why he wanted to get rid of her? Afraid that he might get snared by the husband-hunting gold-digger?

Susannah was working herself into a temper, which wasn't like her. She had inherited a placid nature from her mother and a drive for perfection from her father. At the moment, the two were colliding. As she took another sip of brandy to calm her thoughts, Clive returned to sit beside her.

'Susi, I'm really sorry for that outburst. Can you forgive me?' He picked up Susannah's hands and looked, ruefully, into her eyes.

What a pity I'm not attracted to him, was Susannah's fleeting thought. He really is a most charming man.

'Clive, it's ok, really,' she replied. 'But I do need to know something.'

'What? Anything.' He clearly wanted to get their relationship back on an even keel.

'Did Greg put you up to this?'

'What?' His voice had risen again.

'Telling me to go out on my own?'

There was a moment's silence and then Clive sighed, clasping Susannah's hands even tighter. 'Oh, Susi, Susi. No.' As fulsome as his reply was, Clive stopped suddenly.

'But?' Susannah prompted.

'But …hey …' he seemed unable to find the right words.

'But he told you that I'm only searching for a husband, right? And a rich one at that?' Susannah decided in a split second that she had to have the matter out in the open. She liked Clive, as a friend, and she couldn't bear the thought that another man that she had grown fond of had got completely the wrong impression of her.

Clive turned away, clearly not able to meet her eyes. Susannah tugged on his hands that still held hers. 'Well?'

'Yes, he did, Susi. But I didn't believe him. Hey, I know you two have a history. But that's all I know. He hasn't said anything else, believe me.'

'Other than I'm a gold-digger?'

'Oh, heavens! Yes, yes, that's what he said. But I told him I didn't believe him. That it just wasn't the same person we were talking about.'

Susannah believed what Clive was telling her. When she had overheard Greg that afternoon, that was all she had heard as the two men had moved away from her back towards to hotel. She had stayed a while longer, to calm down, before retracing her own steps.

'There was a misunderstanding,' she began to explain slowly. 'Back on the training course.'

'You were on the Fairchild training course?'

'Yes, I was, with Greg. Only he wasn't Greg Fairchild then,' she couldn't help resentment creeping into her voice. 'He was on the course as Greg Chambers.'

'Ah. Incognito.'

Susannah nodded. 'Exactly. No one knew he was the owner's son, heir to the Fairchild fortune. But he thought that anyone who showed an interest in him could only be interested in his family's money.'

'Oh.' Clive's understanding tone told Susannah she didn't have to explain much more.

'So that's where the gold-digger idea comes from?'

'Yes.'

'But surely he didn't believe that of you? Didn't you get a chance to explain?'

'Me explain?' Susannah exclaimed in righteous indignation. 'I didn't have anything to explain. He most certainly did!'

'Yes, I can see that,' Clive looked sympathetically at Susannah. 'But he's a proud man and perhaps he'd already had experience of fortune hunters.'

He put up his hands in submission as Susannah looked ready to flare up again. But then she subsided back onto the chair and smiled.

'You're probably right,' she admitted. 'I must admit I hadn't thought of it from his point of view.' She was about to add that he hadn't given her a chance and had never even got in touch about her father's accident. But before she could speak again, she found herself enveloped in another of Channing's hugs, big but gentle, and immensely comforting.

'I vote we don't talk about Greg again on this trip,' he suggested. 'If he doesn't know how lucky he is to have such a clever, intelligent expert and, may I say, absolutely beautiful

84

assistant, then it's his downfall. I certainly do and I'm going to do everything I can, Susi, to persuade you to become Mrs Clive Channing the Third!'

At his words, delivered in what Susannah had come to know as his most teasing tone, the two of them collapsed in laughter.

'Well, at least I've been given fair warning,' Susannah said, thinking regretfully once again what a shame it was that the chemistry wasn't there between her and Clive, and that any chemistry there may have been with a certain other gentleman was well and truly wasted.

Chapter 15

'Sorry, Miss Susannah. But Mr Greg is not here tonight.' Susannah was halted in her tracks towards Greg's office by Samuel on reception. She and Clive had just returned from their safari trip. She had turned down his offer of a drink, saying she needed to catch Greg before dinner. But her intentions were clearly to be thwarted.

'Not here?' The surprise showed in her voice. The hotel was the busiest it had been since Susannah's arrival and she couldn't believe that Greg had just left, leaving no one in charge. She went over to the desk and waited while Samuel dealt with a guest who had mislaid his key and a couple who wanted to book places on a day trip to Mombasa later in the week.

'Not here?'

'No, Miss Susannah,' Samuel beamed as he turned his attention to her. Fatherhood had made so much difference to this young man, Susannah had discovered. Now that his wife and child were back home and thriving, Samuel had become one of Susannah's successes. He had taken to heart her words about how important the reception was – the public face of the hotel.

'Mr Greg has taken one of the new guests to the Majestic for the evening.'

'Oh, has he?' Susannah didn't realise she had spoken the words out loud.

'Yes, ma'am,' Samuel nodded. 'The dining-room was pretty full last night. But everything was ok,' he added quickly, seeing alarm spread across her face. 'The extra waitresses you found did just fine.'

Susannah breathed a sigh of relief. It had taken some persuading to get Greg to pay for additional staff – just one of the problems that she had identified in her first few weeks.

'So, he's out?' Susannah didn't want to analyse why she was so anxious to know why he wasn't there.

'Oh, there's Miss Rosalie. She'll be able to tell you,' Samuel said as Greg's secretary came hurrying out of the office, stopping when she saw Susannah.

'Oh, I'm so glad you're back. Did you have a good safari?' Rosalie looked harassed but she brightened on seeing Susannah.

'I did, yes, thank you. It's very busy tonight, isn't it? Where's Greg?' Susannah led the young woman to a seat.

'Oh, he's gone out,' Rosalie's tone of voice alerted Susannah at once.

'A businessman, I suppose, that he wants to impress.' That would be the only reason Greg would take a guest to the Majestic, their competitor.

'Sorry?' Rosalie looked puzzled. 'I hear he's taken a guest to the Majestic.'

'Oh,' Greg's secretary seemed flustered. 'Yes, he has. But it's not a businessman. It's …. it's that model. You know, the one I was telling you about. Eshe.'

Susannah could not believe what she was hearing. A busy hotel and he takes time off with a top international model, leaving the place without anyone in charge.

'She's come back?'

'Yes. Her manager phoned two days ago, the day you and Mr Channing left on safari, and asked for a room for three weeks. It seems that she's stressed and needs a relaxing time out. His words, not mine,' Rosalie giggled.

'Is she still after Greg?' Susannah hated herself for asking. But it seemed so strange that after rejecting Eshe's advances, according to Rosalie, Greg was now taking her off for an intimate dinner at the Majestic's Bistro. Perhaps he thinks it'll work more magic tonight than it did the other night, she thought. Only it sounds as though he won't have so much persuading to do.

A burst of laughter from a group of guests at reception made Susannah look up. Eight ladies were giving Samuel a bit of a hard time.

'Greg said….' Rosalie started to speak.

'Yes?' Susannah turned back.

'Sorry, but Greg said you were to look after that group particularly. They're a bit demanding and loud with it. They seem to want entertaining every minute of the day.'

Susannah sighed. Her break away from the hotel, her job and her responsibilities was clearly over. It was back to earth with a bump. Instead of the peaceful evening she'd envisioned – typing up her report and perhaps even a quiet drink with Clive – all that would have to be put on hold.

'We've a dozen extra guests, too.' Susannah suddenly realised that Rosalie sounded tired.

'A dozen extra? How come? Why?' No wonder the place felt as though it had been invaded. This was definitely the most there had been at the Sunset Beach for months, if not years. Rosalie named a hotel twenty miles the other side of Mombasa.

'One of their water tanks burst,' she explained. 'All their electrics went, several rooms were flooded. The kitchen and dining-room were affected as well. The manager phoned in a panic yesterday morning and Greg said he could bring them all down here.'

'What?' Susannah could only imagine what Greg had been thinking, what with his assistant manager having taken her own 'time out' as he had put it.

'He was actually quite good,' Rosalie said, lowering her voice. 'He asked for your file, you know the one with all the staff details in.'

Susannah hadn't thought Greg was paying any attention to her when she had instigated a more organized filing system and had tried to explain it to him.

'He phoned around, getting those waitresses you'd interviewed and a few extra room staff.' 'He did?' Susannah couldn't believe what she was hearing.

'Oh, yes. He said that I had enough to do, sorting out the rooms and the paperwork. Samuel was great and Peter, too,' Rosalie turned away, but not before Susannah saw a smile appear on her face. She'd thought that those two had been getting quite friendly.

'So, twelve extra guests, eight loud ladies and …'

'And a partridge in a pear tree!' Both girls jumped as a face appeared behind them.

'Oh, Clive!'

'Looks as though there's been plenty going on while we've been away, Susi.'

'Yes, it does, doesn't it?' Susannah reluctantly pushed herself up of the seat. 'I'd better go and sort out those ladies before Samuel resigns,' she joked, looking at the reception desk where the group was still causing havoc.

'Look, why don't you let me do that?' Clive intervened. 'I don't suppose you've even unpacked yet, have you? And there's that report you wanted to get done for Greg. Yes?'

Susannah nodded.

'Well, then. You take a couple of hours. I'll entertain the ladies, and you come and find us. I'll have them softened up by then.' Clive gave Susannah a friendly kiss on the cheek and marched off purposefully towards the group of laughing ladies.

'Oh, so you did have a good time on safari?' Rosalie gave Susannah a friendly nudge.

'It was good,' Susannah confessed. 'He's a very good companion,' she added, emphasising the final word. The two girls smiled at each other and went their separate ways.

An hour and a half later and Susannah was back in the swing. A shower had taken off the safari dust and refreshed her body while a quick meal and a long cool drink had satisfied the inner woman. She spent twenty minutes finishing off her report with the computer in her room and was now on her way to the office to get it printed and ready for Greg in the morning. Then she really must go and rescue Clive from the ladies.

But as she walked past the lounge, Clive spotted her and waved her over to where he was surrounded by definitely more than eight women. He really was a brick, Susannah thought. He must be just as tired as her after their long day, but he had come to her rescue and was still going strong.

'Hi, let me introduce you to all these lovely ladies.' Clive obviously had them eating out of the palm of his hand as they all giggled as if on cue at his words as Susannah approached. 'This, ladies, is your safari expert, the Sunset Beach Hotel's assistant manager, my friend Susi.' He got up, put an arm round her shoulders and led her to a seat in the midst of the group.

As a couple of them started talking to her, Clive put up a warning hand. 'Now, Susi, I've told them that you've been out working all day and that you'll be happy to have a proper talk with them tomorrow, to organise their trips and everything. Is that okay?'

Susannah could only throw him a grateful look and nod in agreement. For a moment she had thought she was going to be kept up all night.

'Clive's been telling us all about the wonderful safaris we can go on,' one of the ladies said, getting her claim in first. 'What we want to know is all sorts of things, like what clothes we'll need to take, where we'll be staying, what animals we'll be seeing …'

She stopped in mid-sentence as once again Clive wagged a friendly finger in front of her. 'Oh, sorry. It's just

90

that we're so excited about it. Your boyfriend has been singing your praises.'

'I tell you what,' Susannah replied, not at all sure how to respond to the boyfriend remark. 'Why don't I say that I'll give a talk tomorrow morning, explaining all about the safaris. Then you can ask all the questions you want. How's that?'

The ladies happily agreed, and Susannah said she would put a notice in reception to let them know where and when. Clive pressed a drink into her hand and managed to squeeze himself between her and the most vociferous of the crowd.

'How do you do it?' Susannah managed to whisper to him at one point when the ladies' attention was momentarily elsewhere.

'It's my natural charm, Susi dear,' he joked.

'Where did the others come from?' she asked. 'I knew we had that party of eight from England, but there's almost double that number here.'

'I think they're from that other hotel, the one with the water troubles,' Clive replied. 'They just seem to have melded together.'

'Perhaps we can pack them off on a few trips together?' Susannah suggested quietly.

Eight would have been a handful, but sixteen were verging on the unruly. No wonder Greg had given in and taken the easy option out.

'I promise I'll get everything organised for tomorrow and we'll take it from there,' Susannah said as she got up. She was more tired than she had thought, and she still had her report to print out for Greg.

Extricating herself from the group took a little more time and as she left the lounge, Susannah made sure she spoke to a few of the other guests; she didn't want anyone to feel left out of the Sunset Beach's hospitality. She made her way to the office. Rosalie must have left the light on for me, she thought, and pushed open the door.

'Oh, excuse me!' Susannah backed out quickly. She hadn't expected anyone to be there at this time of night and she certainly hadn't expected them to be in an embrace! She turned and almost ran out of the reception area and back to her room. The report could clearly wait until morning. Greg obviously had his hands full tonight.

Chapter 16

Next morning, Susannah approached the office cautiously and was relieved to find it empty. She had purposely got up early, although another half hour in bed would have been just the thing. She started up Rosalie's computer and put her disc in, finding her safari report and printing out a couple of copies. Just as she went to put one on Greg's desk, she heard a voice behind her.

'Forgive me,' the tone was anything but regretful. 'But isn't this my office?'

Susannah turned round to find Greg just inches away, towering over her. Normally, she knew, she would have backed away like a mouse, apologising profusely. Not anymore, she decided.

'Yes, it is and that's why I'm here,' Susannah's tone was businesslike. 'Here's my report on my working safari. It was very interesting, very useful. I've made a suggestion that you might like to go and meet some of the lodge managers: great PR for the hotel. All were glad to know that we're back in business, by the way.'

'Well, I'm happy that you were having a good time while we were snowed under here,' Greg took the report out of Susannah's hands. 'What's with the meeting in the lounge this morning? Not more free drinks, I hope? Is that your answer to all our problems?'

He wasn't going to let her forget that, was he? Susannah bristled but then let the remark go. Instead she showed him another page that she'd just printed out.

'I heard when I got back about the unexpected guests,' she said. 'So I've got a few extra things planned for them. I can probably get one or two safaris organised for this week. The fashion show is arranged for Friday and I'll do one or two talks myself.'

Greg nodded, his eyes glancing down the list she had given him.

'But I think another cocktail party might be a very good idea,' Susannah couldn't stop the devil in her making the suggestion.

'Susannah, really. That costs!' Greg replied with a dismissive wave of his hand.

'Does it, Greg?' Susannah heard herself question him, about money. 'If we have a cocktail party tonight, all the new guests will get to know the ones already here; they'll make friends and they'll form little groups for the entertainments we have lined up for the rest of the week. That's when we'll make money – and all for the cost of a few cocktails.'

Greg studied Susannah for what seemed like an age. 'Oh, I get it,' he said finally. 'Clive has been putting ideas in your head.'

'Clive is a businessman who might well invest in the hotel.' Susannah couldn't decide what had made her more cross: Greg refusing to believe that she could come up with any money-making ideas on her own, or the way he had to refer to Clive all the time.

'Leave that to me, Susannah,' Greg's tone was sharp now. 'That's my side of the business. You stick to yours.'

'That's a yes for the cocktail party, then?' It sounded more like a statement and Susannah gave him no chance to respond. 'Let's say 6 'til 8. If you can spare ten minutes for your other guests, I'm sure they'd like to hear from you.'

Susannah knew she'd overstepped the mark and she waited only a split second before side-stepping her boss and making for the door.

'Morning, Miss Susannah, Mr Greg,' Rosalie's bright greeting effectively ended any further conversation as did Greg's shutting of his office door, none too gently.

'What's up with him this morning?' Rosalie murmured to Susannah.

94

'Oh, he just doesn't like spending money,' she replied with a smile. 'But that's exactly what we're going to do. Here.'

She handed Rosalie the list. 'This is what we're putting on in the next couple of weeks, starting with a talk this morning at 11 in the lounge. I'd be grateful if you could come along because I'm hoping to get our safaris restarted this week. I'd like to see Peter immediately after breakfast, please. We're having a cocktail party tonight and he's just the man to organise it.'

She was absolutely beautiful, Susannah acknowledged. Totally and absolutely beautiful. She, Clive, Mildred and Homer had just been introduced to Eshe. The cocktail party was in full swing, everyone mixing well, the noise level constantly rising. She and Clive had been chatting to Mildred and Homer when they had been joined by Greg and Eshe. As tall as Greg, she looked every inch the super model she was. And her dress. Susannah was wearing her sunset dress, the one that had wowed Clive on safari. But next to Eshe, she felt like an over-dressed peacock. The Kenyan beauty was wearing a very plain, simply-cut ivory silk shift that complemented her coffee-coloured skin, showing off her long legs to perfection.

Oh, goodness! Susannah gave a start. I can't be jealous, surely? Not of her, just because she's gorgeous and she's with Greg?

'Anything wrong, Susi?' Clive was all concern at Susannah's expression.

'No, no, it's fine. I'm just thinking of the time.'

She turned to Greg. 'Would you like to say a few words and then encourage everyone into dinner?'

'Already?'

'Well, it is almost eight. Then we won't have to serve any more free cocktails,' Susannah said, knowing that would

95

appeal to his business sense. Greg scowled but did as requested. He was a good speaker when he put his mind to it, Susannah acknowledged to herself. He hit just the right note, commiserating with the guests who'd had to move, welcoming them and others to the Sunset Beach. He had a special welcome for Eshe, which she clearly enjoyed, and he even had a surprise for Susannah.

'I'm not going to hold up dinner too much longer,' he joked. 'I just wanted to thank my staff here at the hotel for the extra work they've been putting in.' His words were greeted with genuine applause. 'Especially my entertainments manager, Susannah over there,' much to her embarrassment he pointed her out, 'she's been working particularly hard on organising extra entertainments for you all. So I hope you'll be signing up for those. That's all from me. Have a good evening.'

'Thank you, Greg,' Susannah waylaid him as he crossed the lounge.

'That's okay, Miss Susi,' he almost laughed in her face with the emphasis on Clive's nickname. 'We have to show a united front here, after all. You've clearly got Clive well-trained: he's been telling me just what a treasure I have in my assistant manager.'

Susannah was furious. Greg made it sound as though she had put Clive up to it. Greg clasped her arm. 'Now, now, don't get in a temper. He's obviously besotted.'

She was just about to vehemently deny any such a situation when Eshe joined them.

'You really do have some lovely ideas, Susannah,' she said, smiling warmly. 'I told Greg so. Being a man, he just wouldn't have thought of a fashion show or shopping trips. But the ladies are thrilled.'

She turned to Greg. 'Why don't the four of us have dinner together, sweetie?'

Sweetie? Susannah couldn't suppress a grin, which she covered quickly with a cough. When Greg didn't answer immediately, Eshe turned back to Susannah. 'Would that be all right? Your boyfriend said he was going to drag you out of the office tonight.'

Susannah could sense rather than see Greg's eyebrows rise, but she could find no excuse. When Clive returned to claim Susannah, the four of them, at Eshe's insistence, went in together to dinner.

'So, can I help in any way?'

Susannah couldn't help liking her. She was really nice. The two of them were having coffee in Mombasa. Normally, Susannah wouldn't have thought of going on one of the days trips with the guests – she had too much to do at the hotel, and as far as Greg was concerned, it would smack of another 'time out'. But when Eshe suggested it, in front of the boss, he'd had little option but to say what a good idea it was.

At least it had given Susannah the opportunity of seeing how the day trips were going. The guide turned out to be popular and knowledgeable. He made sure the ladies had their shops to visit while he had found suitable bar stools where the men could comfortably wait for them. Eshe knew Mombasa well and she had been more than happy to mix in with everyone, suggesting particular shops to visit, advising on purchases, recommending cosmetics.

She wasn't at all stand-offish, Susannah thought, as many celebrities might have been. Here she was, a top international model, offering to help with Susannah's very small and very amateur fashion show. Girls from a local college course had made the clothes and were going to model them. They would just love it if they had Eshe to help.

'I could do a commentary, if you like?' she volunteered, and Susannah jumped at the chance. She herself couldn't have done justice to a job like that and, although Clive had offered, she was quite certain that his expertise didn't stretch to haute couture.

'But this is supposed to be a holiday for you,' she felt she had to give Eshe the chance to have second thoughts.

'Oh, it is, believe me,' she laughed. 'The worst thing about my job is all the travelling. I'm forever in and out of aeroplanes and cars. This is definitely a holiday.'

'Well, if you're sure,' Susannah agreed. 'We're having a run through at the hotel on Thursday afternoon when I think most of the ladies will be doing other things. The show's going to be on Friday evening. Is that okay?'

'Of course,' Eshe smiled. 'I'll let Greg know. He said something about a trip to Malindi. But that can wait until next week.'

Oh! Susannah just stopped herself from exclaiming out loud. So the boss was going to take some 'time out' with a guest. So much for Fairchild Corporation guidelines, she thought. Then something else struck her. Was he doing it to get back at her for going away with Clive? Surely he couldn't be so childish? But why was she giving it any consideration anyway?

What Greg Fairchild did was entirely his business, and she couldn't care one jot! She still couldn't help but smile at the confident way Eshe clearly had Greg exactly where she wanted him. Well, good luck to her. It would get him out of Susannah's hair and that would definitely be an improvement.

Chapter 17

As they were leaving the coffee shop to return to the coach Susannah noticed a poster on the wall. It was advertising the East African Safari motor rally that was to start from Mombasa at the weekend. Their waitress knew all about it. 'It's a great event,' she told them. 'It's like an all-night party. Even if you're not a car fan, there's plenty of action.'

Susannah thought about it on the drive back to the hotel, mentioning it to a number of guests many of whom, particularly the husbands, expressed an interest. When she had a few minutes, she jotted down some notes: this could be another evening entertainment that the Sunset Beach could offer, something a little out of the ordinary.

That evening, Susannah made sure that she had time to herself. Greg and Clive were talking business at the bar and Eshe had found a local girl to give her a massage and facial. She had even suggested to Susannah that she would report back, in case the hotel ever thought of offering such a service. Another idea. The dance lessons were in full swing. With a group of French men on a fishing trip in for dinner, the single ladies had no shortage of partners.

Susannah typed out her proposal, thinking that Greg would certainly give it more consideration than usual as it was something that would attract the men. She was suggesting that the coach would take the party to where the rally was being started. Susannah had consulted Peter and Samuel who told her of a nearby restaurant that could do drinks and a light buffet if guaranteed a good number of people. Everyone would have a couple of hours, either to stay in the restaurant or really get the atmosphere of the rally. Then it would be back to the hotel for a late-night barbecue on the beach.

Susannah had done the costings and added what she thought was a fair profit. All it needed was Greg's approval and she'd put it into action in the morning.

'I really think you've got a lot of nerve!'

'What?' Susannah spun round. She hadn't heard the door open. But there stood Greg, hands on hips, glaring at her.

'You know what!'

Susannah cast her mind back over her day. There was nothing she could think of that should have upset her boss this much. He was clearly furious and she had no idea why.

'What are you talking about?'

'Eshe!' came the answer. She was still puzzled. As far as she knew nothing had happened to upset their famous guest. True some of the ladies had been a bit star-struck when they had first realised who was staying at their hotel. But especially after the city trip this morning, they realised that she was just like them, on holiday, and they were leaving her alone.

'Oh, come on, Susannah.' Greg clearly couldn't believe that she didn't know what he was talking about. 'The fashion show. Only you could ask the country's top model to help out at some silly, tourist fashion show by a load of schoolgirls.'

The sarcasm in his voice spurred Susannah to respond. 'She offered!'

'Oh, yes?'

'Yes, she did. I'm telling you, Greg, I was as surprised as you when she mentioned it to me. I'd never have approached her: she's on holiday, resting,' she tried not to put too much meaning into that word, 'and, as you say, our little effort is nothing in her world. But she offered, I promise.'

'Well, just see that she gets a chance to enjoy herself,' Greg was calming down.

'I thought that was your job.' The words were out of Susannah's mouth before she could think twice. For a second,

Susannah thought that Greg was really going to let rip at her. But instead he grinned.

'Yes, it seems that is my job, and you don't seem to be having a hard time keeping our American businessman entertained either.'

This time there was no ready retort on Susannah's lips and, to her horror, she found herself blushing. Luckily, Greg didn't notice. He was looking at a paper on his desk.

'What's this?' he asked, picking it up. 'Not more ideas that are going to cost me money?'

Susannah took a moment to catch up with his change of topic. He really was the most irritating man.

'Well, it might make a bit,' she ventured. 'Quite a few of the guests have expressed an interest. It's a local event, something they wouldn't get anywhere else….'

'No!' The cry that came from Greg seemed to fill the whole room and beyond. Susannah looked at his face: he was crimson, his eyes bulging.

'But it's a really good party night, I'm told …'

Again, an almost strangled cry from her boss made Susannah stop. He turned away from her, screwing the paper into a ball. 'It's a bad idea and we're not having anything to do with it,' he shouted.

'But, Greg….' He turned back and threw the ball towards the waste-paper basket, narrowly missing Susannah's head.

'I said no, Susannah. I run this place, you don't. You do what I say. That would make a nice change. Stick to your talks and fashion shows, things you know something about.'

His raised voice echoed around the small office and Susannah was sure she heard people outside.

'All right, all right,' she lowered her voice and backed towards the door. 'I'm sorry. I'm sorry.' She had no idea what she was apologising for. She had never seen Greg in such a temper.

As he turned away from her again, she could almost swear that he had tears in his eyes.

Chapter 18

Greg knew he just had to do it. There was no getting out of it. He had to admit that he was in the wrong and that she was right. Damn her. He hadn't slept. He had tossed and turned all night, not just going over their argument but also over all their times together. He still couldn't get his head round the fact that she had played him for a fool all those years ago. Even now, she still managed to get under his skin. He'd have thought an experienced man like him would have been able to forget her, find someone new. But he hadn't.

Oh, there had been girls a plenty, one a week if he'd wanted. He could have had his pick of the women on the training course, and he'd been targeted by her. Since then, he'd travelled the world and there had been many more women available. Although he had enjoyed a few flings, they had come to nothing, just as he had wanted.

'Mr Greg?' Rosalie's voice finally penetrated his thoughts, and he realised she had been knocking on the office door.

'Yes, come in.' He tried hard not to sound cross. Rosalie was working well now; it wasn't her fault that her friend was getting him all steamed up.

'Miss Eshe is looking for you, sir. She was wondering whether you would join her for breakfast?'

Greg sighed and glanced at his watch. He felt as though he had been up for hours. But it was only nine. He didn't feel much like breakfast; even less like making polite conversation. He had to get things cleared with Susannah. Otherwise he'd be a total wreck all day.

'No, Rosalie. Can you tell her I'm tied up with business, please?'

He tried a smile. Susannah was right, it did work.

'Certainly, Mr Greg. Shall I say you'll see her later?'

Greg knew that he and the model were the talk of the hotel. He'd broken his own rule about not getting involved with a guest. But even that was down to Susannah. If she hadn't got upset that evening they'd gone to the Majestic, and then left all lovey-dovey with Channing the next morning, he wouldn't have looked at Eshe. He'd rejected her obvious advances the previous time she'd been at the hotel. This time, he hadn't.

He nodded his assent to Rosalie but as she turned to leave, he stopped her.

'Have you seen Susannah yet?'

Rosalie looked confused. 'I ... er ....'

'Yes or no, Rosalie,' Greg prompted gently.

'Yes, she is about, Mr Greg. But she told me to tell you she's extremely busy this morning.'

'Right.' Greg couldn't blame his assistant manager for wanting to avoid him. 'Thank you, Rosalie. That's all.'

He would have to find her. He couldn't leave this. He was driving her away. And straight into Clive Channing's arms by the look of things, he thought as he finally spied her. He'd looked all over the hotel to no avail and had covered most of the grounds before finding her. There she was, with the businessman. It had been bad enough having to endure a cosy foursome at dinner the other evening, seeing how attentive Channing was. And Susannah didn't seem to be hating it. She was even giggling at one point, he remembered. Some joke that Channing made had appealed to the ladies and he'd felt quite unsettled at the way Susannah had applauded.

Now he was clearly about to interrupt them. They were too wrapped up in each other's company to have noticed his arrival. He coughed and was somehow pleased to see them both jump at the noise.

'Greg, hiya. How are you this morning?' Clive got up and came over to shake his hand.

'Morning, Channing. Sorry to disturb you.'

'No problem. We're just going over everything for Friday's show. Susi's a stickler for timing everything down to the last second.'

Susannah wasn't looking at him. She shuffled the papers on the table in front of them.

'I was wondering, Susannah, if I could just have a quick word?'

Never had Greg sounded so unsure of himself. She looked up and he was shocked at her appearance. It was clear that she hadn't slept either. But worse, there was no warmth at all in her eyes.

'We are a little busy, Greg,' she said, her tone neutral.

'Yes, yes, I know, Rosalie told me, and I wouldn't interrupt if it wasn't important.'

'Shall I give you five minutes?' Channing suggested.

Greg turned to accept but Susannah forestalled him. 'No, it's quite all right, Clive. Whatever Greg has to say, he can say now, so that we can get on with this.'

Greg noticed Channing's eyebrows rise. Perhaps Susannah hadn't told him about last night?

'I wanted to apologise, Susannah. For my outburst. It was unforgivable.'

Greg paused, aware that both of them were looking surprised, if not downright shocked. 'I had things on my mind,' he knew it was a poor excuse, 'and I shouldn't have taken it out on you.' He stopped. He wanted a reaction, but she was just sitting there, not even looking at him.

'Right,' Susannah finally spoke, again in that disinterested tone. He might have been apologising for passing her the wrong jam. Greg waited for her to say more. But a silence fell over the three of them. Someone had to say something.

'So, if you want to go ahead with that idea, Susannah, that's fine.' He hadn't planned on saying that. He hadn't even given it any thought. But at least it brought a reaction from her.

'Right,' she said again. 'I'll get onto that straightaway, then.'

Only then did she look up at him and her eyes said it all. No anger there certainly, but disappointment and even distress. He couldn't match her gaze and looked away.

'So, sorry to disturb you both. Um, I'm going to be out most of today, but I'll be back later, if you'd like to take the evening off, Susannah?'

'Hey, that would great.' It was Channing who welcomed Greg's offer enthusiastically. 'She certainly deserves an evening off, Greg. What about it, Susi? Remember that little bistro restaurant I heard about? How about we try that tonight?'

Susannah suddenly became animated. She smiled at Clive. It was a warm, genuine smile, Greg noticed. 'What a great idea!'

If the tone was a little forced, Channing certainly didn't notice. 'I'll go and book a table,' he said. 'I'll only be a minute and then we'll get back to work, Susi. Ok?'

'Actually, Clive, I'll come with you,' Susannah got up quickly, gathering her papers together. 'I need to start canvassing for the rally and then I'll have to book the buffet dinner.'

Without another glance at Greg, Susannah picked up her bag and walked back towards the hotel, Clive in her wake.

Chapter 19

'Don't be such a spoil sport!' Greg was getting distinctly rattled by Eshe's constant teasing. She seemed to think that he was at her beck and call all day and all night. She just didn't appreciate that he had a business to run.

That's not really fair, said a little voice in his head. It sounded a lot like Susannah. But he knew it wasn't her, just his conscience. Eshe had, after all, hosted a brilliantly successful fashion show the previous evening. The hotel had been packed out. Greg had never seen so many people there. They had almost run out of chairs but Susannah, bless her, had organised the transfer of the patio chairs at the last minute and nobody had been any the wiser. The college girls had been a revelation, Greg acknowledged to himself. Eshe had been genuinely impressed at their creations and she had spent some time coaching them on the catwalk. The Kenyan model had been a brilliant commentator, giving just the right amount of fashion talk, mixed with personal comments, jokes and anecdotes.

Without his knowledge, Susannah had arranged for a free cocktail for everyone at the show. Did that girl ever learn? But, he conceded, it did seem to have encouraged everyone to carry on in the party spirit afterwards. At one point, Peter had even come up to him and expressed the concern that they might be running out of drink. They hadn't but Greg had been on the phone first this morning to double their usual order.

But now Eshe was really going beyond the limit. He had agreed to accompany her to the motor rally event in Mombasa, but she had decided that they should join the rest of the Sunset Beach party on the coach or rather coaches. He'd only just found out that the response to Susannah's idea had exceeded even her expectations and she had had to hire not just one but two extra coaches to accommodate everyone.

'When you drive, you don't drink,' Eshe was complaining. 'If we go with the others, you can really relax, Greg. Wouldn't that be good, for a change?'

He couldn't argue, he knew she was right. In the end, he gave in. If he could have a drink or two, it might help him forget, he reasoned. But it was hard. Too hard. Everywhere there were reminders: the crowds, the cars, the banners, but mostly it was the fumes that brought it all back. He just couldn't avoid that cloying, acrid smell of diesel that got to the very back of your throat. That's what was bringing back the memories he had been avoiding all these years.

The diesel had spilled when the car crashed and seconds later, the car had gone up in flames. There was nothing anybody could have done. That's what the official inquiry had decided. But Greg had never agreed. He'd always blamed himself.

'Hey, is that you? Is that Greg? Greg Fairchild?' A voice rose above the babble of the crowd and instinctively Greg turned round. Across the heads of the crowd, he vaguely recognised a man, one of the rally organisers in the fluorescent green jackets. He ducked his head and moved away. He couldn't face it, meeting someone from his past, from his and John's past. Hoping the man would think he'd been mistaken, he hurried away from the crowds milling around the rally start point.

'Oh, there you are.' Eshe stood up and blocked his path through the restaurant. 'Come and have some food, Greg. You haven't eaten yet, have you?' All Greg wanted was a drink, a long, stiff one. But in front of the hotel guests, not to mention Susannah and Clive, he knew he couldn't refuse Eshe. He allowed himself to be led to the buffet where Eshe piled a plate for him. When they returned to the table, he found himself taking the only empty place, next to his assistant manager.

'It's going well,' he said to her, hoping he would get more reaction now, in public.

'It is, isn't it?' Susannah turned to face him. She was actually smiling, although he was sure it was at a remark of Clive's rather than his praise.

'Yes, congratulations. You were right. Everyone seems to be here.'

'Yes, I couldn't believe it, either,' Susannah seemed happy to talk to him. 'There are only four couples back at the hotel. I made sure they were being looked after and I gave some of the staff the evening off. A few of them came with us. They'll be plenty of people around for the barbecue later,' she added as she saw Greg's expression.

He was about to protest: this wasn't the way to run a hotel. But he found he didn't have the energy tonight. Anyway, if anything went wrong, it would be down to Susannah. Her idea, her responsibility. He flagged a waiter and ordered a brandy, belatedly inviting Clive to join him. The noise was just getting too much.

Susannah had clearly commandeered the best spot in Mombasa, right opposite the start of the rally. Every two minutes, the public address announced the next competitor, horns and rattles identified the supporters, the car would then gun its engines and, on a hooter, would screech off to the cheers of the ever-increasing crowd. Greg was getting a headache. He thought it was the noise but admitted to himself that not a few brandies were probably also contributing.

He looked at his watch. The coaches weren't due to leave for at least another hour. He couldn't wait that long. They'd probably be held up in traffic queues anyway. He looked around for Eshe. She was having a great time luckily. He knew he hadn't been any sort of company for her. But a girl like that would never suffer from a lack of admirers for long.

He got up and staggered a little. Because of the throng nobody noticed, and Greg decided he would slip away and find a taxi. As he made his way through the restaurant, he saw Susannah at the bar, deep in discussion with the manager. Working, always working. He couldn't fault her.

Suddenly, she looked up, catching Greg staring at her. She came over to him. 'Greg? Are you all right?'

'Yes, yes, or rather no. I'm not,' he said. 'I'm going to get a cab back. Can you tell Eshe for me?'

'Really, Greg, don't you think you ought to tell your girlfriend yourself?' Susannah's tone was one of astonishment.

'I'm not feeling well, Susannah,' he said. 'Eshe is having a perfectly good time without me. So I'm going back.'

He turned away from her and walked out of the restaurant, ignoring what he thought was her plea to wait. He pushed his way through the crowds and eventually found a taxi down an unlit alley, well away from the party. Back at the hotel, he couldn't settle. He tried lying down, but images of the rally kept going through his head and he knew he wouldn't be able to sleep. He got up and went to the bar, pouring himself another large brandy, topping it up to the brim.

He thought he heard voices and ducked behind the bar. But they receded and he realised how ridiculous it would have looked, the half-cut manager of the Sunset Beach hotel hiding behind the bar! I'd better get out of here while I can, Greg thought.

He walked unsteadily through the deserted lounge, out past the pools and into the grounds. Turning a corner, he stopped suddenly: in front of him was the barbecue, nicely glowing, with tables of food nearby. They'll be getting back soon, he thought, and changed direction, soon finding himself in his usual hideaway, among the palm trees flanking the beach. He slumped down against a trunk and took a long sip of brandy. It was certainly making him feel better, he thought.

What he'd feel like in the morning, he didn't much care right now.

Chapter 20

It seemed like only seconds later that Greg woke with a start. His head was thumping, and he had spilled what remained of his generous night-cap on his shirt. In the distance, he could hear sounds of merriment: Susannah's damn barbecue, he remembered. He'd have to wait now for all the revellers to turn in. They couldn't see him in this state. He sat up, his mind wandering back to the scenes in Mombasa earlier in the evening. He could still smell the diesel.

All of a sudden, memories from even longer ago came back and for once, Greg couldn't hold in his emotions. Tears began to fall and instead of doing what he considered to be the manly thing, pulling himself together, he let them come. With his head in his hands, he cried for his brother and for the father he'd lost too. He'd never let himself go like this before, always wanting to be seen as the so-called perfect man, in charge at all times. But now he couldn't stop, even when he was aware of footsteps behind him.

'Greg?'

Unable to stem the tears, he tried to wave the unwelcome visitor away but then he felt someone sit down next to him and put a comforting arm around his shoulders. Eventually, the tears stopped, and he wiped his hand over his eyes, too embarrassed to even find out who his comforter was.

'Here.' The voice in the darkness told him it was Susannah as a handkerchief was pressed into his hand.

He still couldn't look at her. He could smell her perfume, feel the warmth of her arm and the silky softness of her orange-red dress that he loved so much. Without thinking, he turned and buried his head in her arms, his body still shaking with sobs. He felt her arms tighten, one hand stroking his hair.

'What is it, Greg? What is it? Can I help?'

He heard her words and wondered how she could still be so kind, so caring, so loving, considering how he had treated her. He pulled himself away, turning to face the sea, still not wanting to see what was in her eyes. Pity, probably, he reckoned.

'I'm sorry, Susannah.' His voice was shaky. 'Things just got on top of me. I'm sorry if I was rude earlier.'

'That's ok, Greg. It's not a problem. No one noticed. But I thought there was something wrong. Is it something you want to talk about? Can I help?'

That was her, thought Greg as he started to calm down. That was the essence of Susannah, always thinking about other people, caring how they were, wondering if there was anything she could do. Never a thought for herself.

'It was the car rally,' he said and felt her sit up and away from him.

'The car rally?' Her tone was incredulous. 'Are you still on about that?'

'No, no, you've got it wrong. I'm not blaming you or your idea. It's my own fault. I didn't explain. I couldn't. But if you'll hear me out, I will.' Now he turned to look at her and there was only caring in her eyes. Caring and concern.

She looked so lovely, sitting there on the sand, the moonlight just catching her hair and those green eyes, her legs tucked underneath her, one of her dress straps slightly askew. He bent forward and gently slid the strap back onto her shoulder. He thought she might flinch and he wouldn't have blamed her. But she didn't. The night breeze wafted her scent towards him again and he had an overwhelming desire to take her in his arms and kiss her. Perhaps she sensed his thoughts, perhaps not. But she seemed to retreat just a little, leaning back onto the trunk of the tree.

'Well?'

Haltingly at first, Greg told her about John. How the two of them had been the best of friends, going their separate

113

ways at work but spending a lot of their free time together. They each excelled at many sports, but it had been Greg who had taken to car rallying. He competed all over Europe and Africa and then John wanted to join him. He tried to teach him, but John was always the more adventurous of the two, always wanting to be the better, ready to cut corners.

Greg's account became slower and more fractured as he told Susannah what had happened at one of the minor rallies in Uganda five years ago. He himself had pulled out of the event, having had a prolonged bout of flu back. John had insisted on taking his place in the team car. He'd taken the corner too fast, the car had crashed and burst into flames. Marshalls had held Greg back from trying to save his brother.

'Oh, Greg. I understand now. I'm sorry I put you through that.' Susannah's gentle voice was almost more than he could take right now.

He took her hand and held it tightly. 'No way is it your fault,' he said. 'I should have been more up front. It was a success tonight, Susannah, for you and the hotel. There's absolutely no reason why my past, my misdemeanours should get in the way of that.'

'It was hardly your misdemeanour,' she contradicted him.

'Tell that to my father!' All the bitterness came out. 'He blames me for getting John involved in rally driving. He blames me for allowing John to take my place. But I didn't.'

Susannah held his hand tightly; he was getting upset again.

'I knew nothing about it until one of the other members of the team faxed me with the details. They weren't asking any questions - one Fairchild brother taking the place of another – no questions to be asked. It was a Fairchild team.'

'So how can your father blame you, then?'

'Oh, I was the one who had introduced John to rallying, encouraged him to compete, particularly that last rally …'

'That's hardly fair,' Susannah interrupted gently. 'He was an adult, he led his own life. Your father could hardly expect you to be your brother's keeper.'

'You can always see the other side, can't you,' Greg said gratefully. 'You're a very special person, Susannah. I expect your father really appreciates your qualities.'

Susannah looked shocked and opened her mouth to reply to Greg's words. But they were both suddenly aware of a rustle in the trees behind them. Greg got to his feet and helped Susannah to hers, just as a low, sexy voice called out.

'So, this is where you've got to. I didn't know I had to play hide and seek for your favours!'

The branches parted and there stood Eshe, dressed only in a bikini top and sarong, holding a champagne bottle, two glasses and a blanket.

Chapter 21

Greg still couldn't look Susannah in the eye. It was a week now since the rally night and they had barely spoken. They were communicating through Rosalie or via notes left on each other's desks: impersonal notes, neatly typed, business reports really. Susannah was busy organising safaris, day trips and her forthcoming talks; he was keeping busy doing goodness knows what, keeping out of Eshe's way most of the time.

The incident on the beach had turned into a nightmare. He had glimpsed Susannah's shocked expression when Eshe had interrupted their heart-to-heart and she had made her escape as quickly as possible, without so much as a backward glance at the man she had been consoling only minutes earlier.

Eshe had demanded to know what he was up to, standing her up and then being found with another woman in their hideaway! She hadn't noticed Greg's tear-stained face or his troubled demeanour. She had let rip in a most unladylike way, crowning her performance by smashing the champagne bottle against a tree, the contents spraying him all over, joining the already stale odour of spilt brandy.

He apologised the following morning. She wanted an explanation, but no way was he going to confess to another woman. He merely told her that the headache which had come on at the rally had got worse and that he'd been trying to escape the barbecue crowd. Eventually, after several dinners in a more romantic and more expensive setting than the dining room of the Sunset Beach, she had come round and was once more claiming all of his attention.

He knew he was spending more and more of his time in his office nowadays: it was the only place that he could be sure Eshe wouldn't walk in on him, Rosalie would see to that. But work, for the moment, was at a standstill. He had no more potential investors to see, all the reports for head office had been completed and sent off. The hotel was running smoothly. Guests were arriving, staying and leaving with very few, if any, complaints.

'Yes, he's here. No, I don't think he's on the phone. Go on in.'

Greg felt like an animal caught in the glare of headlights, he had no escape route. He lifted the phone and put on an expression of intense concentration. As the door opened, he expected to see the tall, slim and undoubtedly attractive Eshe. But where once he would have been flattered by her insistent attentions, now he only felt irritation. Was he getting old? Heaven forbid!

But it wasn't Eshe. It was the woman who appeared to have been avoiding him, and he her, since that night on the beach. In the split second when he realised who it was, Greg just couldn't explain the feelings that coursed through him.

'Greg, sorry to bother you.' Her voice was brisk, calm and totally businesslike. 'Do you have just a moment, please? I wouldn't normally ask but ...'

Greg quickly put the phone down and turned towards her. 'Susannah, come in. Of course I have time. Here, sit down.' He rose and pulled out a chair, trying to ignore the surprise on her face. Had he never offered her a chair before?

'It's only a quick query,' Susannah sat on the edge of the chair, looking for all the world as though she wanted to make a speedy getaway.

'Shoot.'

She almost jumped out of her chair at his instruction. Was he trying too hard, he thought?

'It's just that ...' she paused.

'Yes?' This sounded like the old Susannah, the shy, hesitant, insecure Susannah. Not the smart businesswoman who had been a godsend to the Sunset Beach Hotel. 'It's just that there's been an accident ...'

117

'What?' Greg leapt from his chair. How could she sit there so meek and mild when there had been an accident!

'With the slide projector.'

Greg was almost certain she was hiding a grin behind those words. How foolish he felt. She was doing it on purpose, to get back at him for the other night.

'Oh, for god's sake, Susannah,' Greg sank back down into his chair and turned so that he was looking out of the window. 'Deal with it. That's your job.'

'Yes, I know. But the bulb has smashed and we haven't got a spare. I'll need to get one sent down from Nairobi, unless …' again she hesitated.

'Unless?'

'Are you going to Nairobi by any chance?'

'Me? No.' Greg turned back and looked at her. Had his assistant manager gone completely mad? She wouldn't meet his eye. 'Why should you say that?'

Susannah got up and made for the door.

'Sit down, Susannah, and explain yourself,' Greg ordered.

'All right.' She snapped back at him and despite himself, Greg smiled.

'So, tell me what's happened,' he suggested, looking directly at her, trying the smiling routine once again.

'We were having a run-through of Saturday's talk, Samuel doing the slides, when there was a loud bang and the lights went out. Don't worry.' Susannah's eyes flashed impatiently as a look of horror crossed Greg's face. 'It's all right. The ground floor fuse went; that's been replaced. But it blew the projector bulb and when we looked in the case, there were no spares. I don't want to do the talk without my slides, and I don't know if we can get a replacement from Nairobi in time.'

'Okay,' Greg nodded. 'That's the bulb. I can sort that. But why did you think I was going to Nairobi? You know I'd have told you if I was going to be away overnight. We're a team, Susannah, like it or not. I'm not that irresponsible.' He didn't know why, and he wasn't about to analyse his feelings right now, but he was anxious that just because his personal life was in a bit of a mess, she didn't think he could handle the business side either.

'Eshe,' came the succinct reply.

'What do you mean?' It took all of Greg's control not to shout at her.

'She said you were going away for a couple of days, to see some people in the capital.'

'She said that?'

'Yes, I just assumed you had more contacts to see, and you were taking her with you …' Susannah's voice trailed off as she caught Greg's expression: he was almost at eruption point.

'Well, we're not and never have been going to Nairobi,' he said, finding it hard to keep his voice down. 'She's a guest, nothing more.'

He wasn't looking at Susannah, but he knew that her highbrows had risen. He couldn't blame her, really. To everyone else at the Sunset Beach, staff and guests, it was clear that he and Eshe had something going. The model made sure she always accompanied him to the bar before dinner and she had even started talking to the other guests as though she was interested in their welfare, just as he and Susannah did. She insisted on eating with him, as and when he stopped by long enough to be persuaded into the dining-room and it seemed that Eshe always made it known when he was taking her to another hotel for a meal. He could hardly blame Susannah for not believing him.

'Right, if you are able to get a new bulb, then I won't cancel the talk,' Susannah was being businesslike again.

119

'Yes, I will. I'll do that today.' He paused and Susannah took the opportunity to get up. This time she got to the door and opened it.

'Susannah, wait.' She looked round at him, again with that quizzical expression. But he had no idea what he wanted to say to her. This was hardly the time, or the place, to discuss their most famous guest.

'It's okay,' he said. 'I'll let you know when I get the bulb.'

'Thank you,' she gave him a half-smile – that was an improvement, he thought – and left.

Chapter 22

'So why do we have to stay here tonight?' Eshe was clearly in a strop and Greg wondered how he was going to win this one. She was making it quite clear that she wanted a meal out and a night of dancing. He sighed. He couldn't really blame her. Whenever they had tried to have an evening by themselves at the Sunset Beach, they had been constantly interrupted by eager guests. At least now those interruptions were more positive ones, Greg realised, and not complaints. There were requests for information, compliments about the hotel, and even the men, usually well into retirement, who were flirting with Eshe.

'Because it's Susannah's first talk and I want to be here,' he replied for what felt like the tenth time that day.

'Why?' Eshe demanded. 'She's the assistant manager here, she's an adult. She's extremely capable. Why do you need to be here?'

Greg was lost for words. In a way Eshe was right: the competent, confident Susannah should be perfectly able to conduct her talk without him. But he was remembering their training course and how Susannah hated to be the centre of attention, standing up in front of the rest of the trainees. More than once the trainers had stopped her to say that she couldn't be heard, to speak up, slow down, put some life into her delivery, make eye contact, all the attributes of a seasoned public speaker. But she had found it hard, and they had both been delighted to celebrate when she had passed the so-called public entertainment part of the course. Greg hadn't been privy to her final presentation, so he was still judging her on her nervous, stumbling practice sessions.

'Because I'm her boss and I want to see her first presentation,' he said to the woman now sulking by his office door. No way was he going to tell Eshe that he wanted to be around just in case Susannah needed back up. He could introduce her and stay beside her, ready to join in if she faltered. The guests could think it was a joint presentation. He could field any awkward questions, and she could stick to what she knew: the safaris. He didn't want her to fail. Once again, Greg refused to analyse his feelings as to why it was so important. For the good of the hotel, he rationalised to himself.

'Really, Greg, you've had hardly any time for me,' Eshe complained. As Greg raised his eyebrows, she changed tack. 'For us, sweetie. I really thought we had something going. This is a lovely place you have here, although it would be nice to see the rest of the Fairchild empire some time?' She came round to Greg's side of the desk, stood close to him and stroked his cheek.

'Eshe, please, I'm working.' The old Greg would never have backed off from such an obvious flirtation: Kenya's top model making very clear advances! But the new Greg was finding he just couldn't cope. He didn't understand it: the thrill of the chase was no longer there; the novelty of a new girlfriend every few months no longer held the appeal it had. What was wrong with him? Business worries, probably, he thought.

'Okay, okay, I'll leave you alone,' she put up her hands in mock surrender and walked away from him. 'I know you've got to make this place a success. But all work and no play …' She left the sentence unfinished as she sashayed provocatively out of his office.

Greg sank back into his chair and took a deep breath. He was going to have to address this particular problem, he realised, and sooner rather than later.

'You are absolutely wonderful!' Clive's voice echoed across the ballroom and Susannah, busy setting up the slide projector, turned and giggled at him.

122

'I shall have to believe it sometime, you tell me so often.'

'Ah, um.' Greg coughed in what he thought was a discreet manner as he came through the doors, his eyes skimming the papers he held. He didn't want them to think he was spying.

'Hey, Greg!' Clive advanced, holding out his hand. They hadn't seen each other for all of four hours and there was that handshake again

'Channing.'

Wherever Susannah was it seemed that nowadays so was Clive and it was beginning to get on Greg's nerves. He had managed to impress on Eshe that he had to work. Why couldn't Susannah do the same? Even as the thought went through his head, he knew he was being unfair. Clive Channing was an important business contact, as well as a hotel guest. Whatever Channing was to Susannah, Greg had never seen the two of them act inappropriately in public. Unlike Eshe, Susannah did not drape herself over her dance partner, nor steal kisses when she thought no one was looking. Was she really serious about the guy? Greg wanted to know. But he wasn't sure why.

'Clive's been helping me with the projector. Are you happy with him doing that this evening, Greg?'

It was as though Susannah was reading his mind. 'Yes, that's absolutely fine, if you don't mind giving up your evening,' Greg was trying to make a light-hearted remark, but he knew full well that Channing would still be in the audience if he wasn't helping the speaker.

'Just trying to be useful, Greg. Hope that's ok with you?'

Was he too reading Greg's mind, asking permission to hang around the assistant manager?

'No problem,' Greg tried to sound friendlier. 'Everything all set?'

'Yes, all ready.' Susannah collected up her notes as Channing switched off the projector.

'I'm just going to have a bite to eat, get changed and then I'll be ready to greet everyone as dinner finishes.' She didn't sound nervous, Greg thought.

'I'll introduce the evening, Susannah,' he said. 'Then you take over.'

'Oh.' She turned to face him, surprise written on her face.

'Is there a problem with that?'

'No, no, of course not,' She was now flustered. 'It's just that I wasn't expecting you.'

'Your first presentation? Of course I'd be here, to support.' Greg didn't want her thinking he was checking up on her.

'Thank you,' Susannah said quietly as Channing joined them.

'Are you sure I can't tempt you with a cocktail, Susi?'

'No, really. I'm fine. I'll see you both in here then at 9:15?'

Greg nodded his agreement and was inexplicably bothered when Clive indicated his with a kiss on Susannah's cheek.

'So, Ladies and Gentlemen, I shall now hand you over to your safari and wildlife expert – Miss Susi.'

Greg moved away from the centre of the stage, conscious of the applause and laughter that had greeted his introduction to the evening. He hadn't intended using Channing's moniker for Susannah. In truth, he detested it; Susannah was a much nicer name. But on his way into dinner that evening, he had heard quite a few of the guests referring to her as 'Miss Susi' and realised that it was now well-established around the hotel.

He looked at Susannah as she walked onto the low platform that had been made into a temporary stage in front of the slide screen. She was wearing his favourite dress: the orangey-red silk that looked like a sunset. Round her throat she wore a light scarf in the same colours that perfectly set off her lightly tanned skin. Pale pink strappy sandals complemented her long slim legs. She looked good. Her face glowed, not artificially he noted with approval. Her tan, rosy cheeks and sparkling eyes with just a touch of pink lipstick was all she needed to look stunning.

Pull yourself together, Fairchild! Greg shook his head, as though waking from a dream. She was his assistant manager, a past love, with the emphasis very much on the past. He couldn't understand his reawakened interest in her. All that was over. She had duped him five years ago and it wasn't about to happen again.

He suddenly felt a hand slip into his and he turned to see that Eshe had made an appearance after all. They had dined together but she had gone off to talk to a party of younger guests who were catching a taxi into Mombasa for the nightlife. He had assumed she had gone with them. But no. Here she was, making up to him again.

'Sorry, sweetie. I haven't missed anything, have I?'

Greg smiled, shook his head and gave her hand a quick squeeze. He wouldn't have blamed her at all for not staying. She wasn't the safari sort and a night on the town was much more her thing than a talk on Kenya's wildlife. So it was good of her to come. He pointed to a couple of chairs against the wall that someone had carefully reserved, the rest of the room was full. They moved quietly to take their seats just as Susannah asked for the lights to be lowered, smiling at her assistant, Clive Channing the Third, to bring up the first slide.

It was only a few minutes into the show when Greg realised just how good Susannah had become. She was perfectly at ease, keeping up a lively commentary with enough but not too much information, no awkward pauses, jokes that the guests could appreciate, and even carrying on a friendly banter with Channing. She didn't even have any notes to refer to, he noticed. Clearly, he had no cause to worry. He wasn't going to have to jump in to cover any embarrassing moments. He could relax and enjoy her talk.

Chapter 23

Almost an hour later, he managed to work his way through the crowd around his assistant manager, passing her a glass of champagne with a nod and a smile. The show had been planned to last twenty minutes but when Susannah finished her commentary and the lights went up, she was inundated with questions: mostly about the safaris, some about the animals, and some even about her own personal situation. Where did her love of animals come from? Where had she grown up? Where did she go to university? Far from being embarrassed, which the old Susannah certainly would have been, the new Susannah coped brilliantly, deflecting the personal questions with answers that led to another anecdote or a subtle change of subject.

'Here you are, Susi.' Greg deliberately used the nickname, just to see her reaction. Smiling, she grimaced at him, took a long sip and let out a sigh.

'Do you think it was all right?'

'All right? No, I do not.' Greg could have kicked himself for trying to make a joke out of her anxious query. Susannah's face clouded over and for a split second, he almost thought he could see tears in her eyes.

'Hey, it was brilliant. I was making a joke. It wasn't just all right, it was brilliant.'

Susannah turned away from him and he could see that she was passing the back of her hand over her eyes. It must have been an ordeal and here he was, making light of it.

'Susannah, I'm sorry. Really, believe me, it was one of the best talks I've ever heard. You had them in the palm of your hand. They loved it. Come on, let's get out of here. Leave that.' He took her arm as she moved towards the slide projector. 'Let Peter do that. You've done enough tonight. Come on, come and enjoy your success.'

127

But instead of complying with his request, Susannah all but wrenched her arm away from his gasp. The next moment, she was in floods of tears.

'Susannah?' Greg couldn't have been more shocked. He glanced towards the door and was relieved to see the last of the guests moving into the lounge. He put his arm lightly round Susannah's shoulders and drew her towards him. This time, she didn't resist. He held her close, lightly but, he hoped, comfortingly. He couldn't believe he had upset her so.

'Here,' he pressed his handkerchief into her hand and let her wipe her eyes. Gently, he lifted her chin. Her face was tear-stained and she wouldn't look up at him. He stroked her cheek and very slowly, bent towards her. At the last second, her eyes lifted to meet his and all he wanted to do was to blot out the pain he saw there. Their lips met and the past five years melted away. Susannah was in his arms again and he never wanted to stop kissing her. His hold tightened and he felt her lean into him. They broke away for a second, their eyes locked, their lips wanting more. This time, the kisses deepened and all Greg's old feelings for the girl in his arms resurfaced. He moaned and held her still tighter.

'So let's find those two workaholics and insist they have a celebratory drink.'

The door burst open and Clive's loud voice preceded him and Eshe, giving Greg and Susannah just enough time to break apart.

'There you are. Come on, work's over for tonight. Leave all this. We're celebrating!'

Susannah turned away, giving herself a moment to dab at her eyes, while Greg grabbed at the projector, hoping it looked as though he had started packing it away. Someone had to say something.

'Congratulating Susannah, were you?' Eshe filled the silence.

'Yes, yes, I was,' Greg's voice sounded unsteady to his ears but the others didn't seem to notice.

'Absolutely.' Channing's enthusiasm was grating now. All Greg wanted to do was to get away and take Susannah with him. But he knew he could hardly do that here and now. He gave himself a mental shake and forced commonsense to prevail.

'Right, we're coming. I'll get Peter to sort this. All right, Susannah?' He was concerned. She hadn't said a word and was still dabbing at her eyes. Surely he couldn't have upset her that much?

'Sorry, got something in my eye,' Susannah's words came out muffled. 'Here, let me …'

The two men spoke at the same time and it was Clive who reached Susannah's side first.

'It's ok now,' Susannah said quickly. 'Thank you.'

'Come on then, Susi. I've got a table waiting and a bottle of champagne,'

Clive took charge, guiding Susannah with an arm around her shoulders. Greg could do nothing but watch them go.

'And what was that touching little scene all about?'

Greg swung round, not at the words, but at the tone of Eshe's voice. Her expression matched the suppressed anger.

'What are you talking about?' Greg tried to sound nonchalant as he began dismantling the projector.

'Don't mess around with me, Greg,' the anger was less suppressed now. 'Something was going on and I'm fed up with being strung along like this.'

Greg sighed and faced her. 'I wasn't aware that I've been stringing you along, Eshe,' he said. 'I thought, in your words, we were having a bit of fun. I've never promised you anything else. I enjoy your company. But …'

His next words were cut off sharply as the sound of a slap echoed around the room. Greg put a hand up to his face. In truth, he couldn't blame her. He'd soon realised that she was keener than he. But now, he just didn't want to know. He was in turmoil, but he knew it wasn't Eshe that was the cause of that feeling.

'It's Susannah, isn't it?'

Was she reading his mind? 'What?'

'Susannah. Your assistant manager.' Eshe made it sound almost obscene. 'You've got history, haven't you?'

'I don't know what you're talking about …'

'Oh, don't give me that, Greg. I caught you the other day, on the beach at midnight, when we were supposed to be meeting. If you and Susannah have something going, why pick on me for light relief? Because she's going to dump you?'

Greg was about to retort that it had been Eshe who had picked on him. But then he became aware of her final words: Susannah going to dump him?

'I have no idea what you are talking about,' he said firmly. 'Susannah works for me and that's it. Believe what you like, Eshe. I really don't care.'

130

He heard a movement and realised that she had turned and walked back towards the door. She stopped and looked at him. He thought it was pity he could see on her face.

'You really don't know what's going on under your nose, do you, Greg? I watched you tonight. You didn't see a single one of those slides, did you? You were watching her, the whole time.'

Greg changed his mind about the pity: it was bitterness, pure and simple.

'Well, whatever you've got going, or think you've got going, it's not going to last long.'

'What do you mean?' In spite of himself, Greg had to ask. He wasn't up to guessing games this evening.

'She's leaving, Greg. Clive Channing the Third might not have your looks, but he has a hell of a lot more charm and Susannah's fallen for it. Hard.'

Chapter 24

Thank goodness Greg was away for the day! Perhaps she could sort herself out while he was gone, and everything could get back to normal. Normal? What was normal? Susannah knew she was kidding herself. Nothing about her and Greg was normal, especially after last night. The attraction between them was still there – obviously. So what was she going to do about it? What was he going to do about it?

Those were the questions that had been spinning round her head virtually all night and she was definitely feeling the worse for wear. It hadn't been the champagne. She had resisted Clive's entreaties to help him finish their celebratory bottle but even so, it had taken her a long time to drop off to sleep, only to wake every few hours with her mind buzzing.

At five o'clock, she instinctively knew she was fully awake, so she got up and went for an early morning swim, a walk away down the beach. She certainly didn't want to bump into any other early risers. But when she returned to the hotel, it was to be greeted with the news that the manager had left early, gone out for the day and not to expect him back much before dinner.

Susannah welcomed a day's reprieve from that particular problem, but she had plenty to do. One group of guests was leaving at lunchtime, and another was arriving in the late afternoon. Oh, and the newcomers' welcome party, she'd have to host it on her own. The parties had become an established part of the Sunset Beach's routine: one every five or six days at which all guests were welcome, but which really gave the new arrivals a taste of Kenyan hospitality. These ran these like clockwork now: Greg doing the big welcome, Susannah adding the details. Perhaps she could enlist Clive's help again, like the first day they had arrived. That seemed so long ago now. Then, she hadn't even known Greg was the manager and now, he just wouldn't leave her thoughts.

'Hey, Susi.' Clive's distinctive tones sounded across reception and Susannah halted on her way to the office.

'Clive, good morning.'

'So, have you time for our lunch in Mombasa?'

'Oh, Clive!' Susannah had completely forgotten that he had suggested lunch out today, a reward for her wonderful performance at the slide show.

'I can't. Greg's away for the day, apparently. I've got to see to the new arrivals and host the cocktail party tonight.'

'Greg's away? He didn't say anything last night.'

'No, he didn't. I don't know any more than that. A business meeting, I suppose,' Susannah responded. Clearly Clive didn't know any more than her.

'No, it's not a business meeting.' Susannah and Clive spun round at the words, softly spoken by Rosalie in the doorway of Greg's office.

'Why's he away then? It's not an emergency is it?' Susannah queried.

'Well, she made it sound like an emergency,' Rosalie said beckoning the two of them into the office, away from the people gathering in reception. Susannah knew she really didn't need to ask the question.

'Eshe's taken him on a day out?'

Really! On one of the busiest days of the week and he takes time out with that woman – and after what had happened last night too. She could feel her temper rising, and she wasn't usually a fiery person.

'No, not a day out. She's leaving.'

'Leaving?' This time it was Clive asking. 'Why? I thought she was staying another week.'

'She was. But last night she came looking for me. It was after your slide show, Susannah. She seemed very worked up about something. She asked me to get her on a flight today.

I said I would arrange a car for her too but she told me not to. She said Greg was taking her to the airport.'

'Greg doing a taxi run?' Susannah could hardly believe her ears.

'Oh, it wasn't his choice,' Rosalie said. 'I heard her. She said he owed her and that was that.'

Susannah suddenly became very interested in the morning's post which lay unopened on her desk. She turned away from the others and started sorting through the pile. 'Oh, well. I suppose we'd just better get on with it. Rosalie, could you check with Peter that everything's okay for the party this evening? Clive, I'm sorry, but I'm going to be busy all day.'

She realised her words sounded like a dismissal but right at this moment, she had to be on her own. She needed a large black coffee and some breathing space.

Susannah soon found that her words were prophetic. She was extremely busy all day, leaving her very little time to think, let alone sit and contemplate what she was to do about Greg. The weather over the past few days had been unseasonably hot, even for the east coast of Kenya. By mid-morning, many of the staff were predicting a massive storm.

'I think we should clear all the furniture from the patios,' Peter said when Susannah went to consult him. 'The wind's getting up and I don't think it'll be safe.'

'Right. Let's do it now, before it gets worse.' Susannah made the decision and within twenty minutes, all the outside areas had been cleared. The few guests who had been sitting round the pools had been told of what was expected and they had come inside, quite happy to sit on the open terrace, drinks at hand.

During the morning Susannah heard from Samuel that the departing guests had reached the airport safely and within the hour he phoned again to say that the new group had landed and they were just leaving for the hotel. Thirty minutes later, the storm broke. To begin with it seemed just like the normal daily shower: a quick, heavy downpour, all over in ten minutes or so, leaving the air pleasantly warm and fresh. But this time, the rain just kept on coming.

At first, the guests who had been happily ensconced on the terrace enjoyed the experience. But over the next hour, the wind got up and, blowing off the sea, forced the guests back into the hotel. Any chairs that hadn't been stacked securely away were blown into the swimming pools and loose items from the beach found their way into the hotel grounds – branches, towels, Tshirts, even a brightly-coloured water bed.

Susannah was pacing the reception hall, trying not to show that she was getting worried about the incoming guests. The road from Mombasa had been improved in the past couple of years but even so, there were one or two places where it crossed what were usually small streams. Goodness knows what state they'd be in now. Susannah thanked her lucky stars that she had insisted that Greg hire a sturdier vehicle for the airport transfers. The dilapidated old bus she and Clive had been greeted with had been retired and they now hired minivans and coaches as they needed them. Greg had argued, she remembered, about the increased cost, but he had given in. Now, she thought, he ought to be thankful.

'They've arrived.' Rosalie's words brought a sigh of relief from Susannah. She rushed out to welcome the new arrivals. She could see immediately that a party of four elderly ladies looked quite shaken.

Samuel managed a quick whisper, 'The rivers have burst their banks, Miss Susi. We were driving through a foot of water at times.'

Between them, Susannah and Rosalie got all the guests into the hotel and settled into the lounge with welcoming drinks, many asking for a pot of tea: that ubiquitous panacea in times of stress. Susannah made an impromptu speech, anxious that they weren't getting a completely wrong impression of their holiday destination.

She noticed that Clive had reappeared: he seemed to make himself scarce after Susannah's outburst at the start of the day and when she'd had five minutes, she had gone looking for him to apologise. But here he was, charming the guests as ever, paying particular attention to one elderly gentleman who looked a little worried.

'Miss Susi will sort out anything you need, sir,' she heard him say.

'But where's the manager?' came the rather irate reply.

'Oh, he's just away for a few hours on business, sir,' Clive was quick with the excuse. 'But Miss Susi, she's an excellent assistant manager. Just between you and me,' Susannah saw Clive bend down to the guest, 'She runs this place, and you won't be sorry you chose the Sunset Beach.'

Susannah smiled warmly as Clive looked her way and she went over to join them, adding her reassurances to Clive's. 'Hello, sir. I'm Susannah. Let me welcome you to the Sunset Beach.' She shook hands with the man, noting that he did seem to be calmer now.

'Is it usually like this?' he asked, in a more reasoned tone, gesturing at the rain outside that was still hammering against the windows.

'No, it's not,' Susannah confirmed. 'In October we're supposed to have what they call the 'little' rains. This is much more like our main rainy season in May. But I'm told that it will all be over today and that everything will get back to normal next week.' She smiled and was pleased to see his eyes brighten.

'I'll show the gentleman to his room, if you like, Susi?' She could sense that Clive was testing out the waters and didn't want to overstep the mark.

'Of course, Clive. That would be really nice of you,' she responded, reluctantly turning away as another guest came up to claim her attention.

Chapter 25

By dinner time the winds had died down, but the rain was as relentless as ever, filling the swimming pools to overflowing and making quagmires of the flowerbeds. Several times during the evening Susannah's thoughts had turned to Greg: surely he wouldn't drive back through this? Several members of staff had come to work with tales of local roads having become impassable because of flooding, mudslides and fallen trees. Those who lived on the other side of the inlet at Cannon Point had never arrived. Clearly, the ferry wasn't running. Guesthouses just up the road, barely a mile away, had lost their electricity and the Sunset Beach had taken in more unexpected guests.

At least we have a working generator, Susannah thought, touching wood for luck. The hotels along the Indian Ocean were used to emergencies like this in May when severe weather was often expected. But in October, this was way out of the norm.

'Miss Susi? I think we'd better close the garden terrace.' Peter's anxious words broke into Susannah's thoughts as she stared out of the office window. She turned and saw him in the doorway.

'Yes, of course, Peter. Do that. There should be room in the main lounge. Is everything all right in the dining room?'

'Yes, Miss,' Peter reassured her. All available staff had been drafted in to help in the kitchen and dining room. Susannah knew quite a few of them had already worked their normal shifts and were staying on. Some of them had no choice; they knew they couldn't get home tonight and another of Susannah's jobs had been to organise makeshift dormitories. She had taken over a couple of spare rooms that were on the list to be refurbished when the hotel was really back on its feet.

Making her way through the lounges, Susannah found herself constantly reassuring the guests, new and old, that this was indeed extreme weather that wouldn't be lasting for long and yes, the Sunset Beach, did have its own electricity supply. Inwardly, she was praying that she wasn't tempting fate. But on the whole, she also felt that the guests were enjoying the experience of something out of the ordinary. There was a sense of camaraderie with the new arrivals being taken in by established groups.

Peter had suggested putting on some tapes that the band had left so that those who wanted to could have a dance, and this too was going well in the other lounge. Susannah gave a quick wave to Mildred and Homer on the far side of the room. Normally she would join them for a few minutes. They were seasoned Africa travellers and they had plenty of tales to tell. But after her efforts all day, Susannah was beginning to feel just a little tired. Perhaps she could sneak away for an hour and return later.

But no sooner had the thought entered her head, she was lightly grasped by the elbow. She turned and found Clive smiling at her.

'Come and join us for a drink, Susannah,' he said. 'You've done quite enough for today. Everyone's settled,' he indicated the groups of contented people in the lounge, 'and they've asked quite enough questions for tonight.'

What a nice, thoughtful man he was, Susannah thought. Quite unbidden, another came into her head. Why couldn't she have fallen in love with someone like Clive? So much more straightforward than Greg. Without warning, tears came to her eyes and she had to stop in her tracks.

'What's up, Susi?'

'Oh, just something in my eye,' she managed to say, brushing away the tears. Clive took her by the arm and led her to a seat in the corner of the lounge where he had an umbrella-

139

laden cocktail waiting for her. The elderly gentleman Clive had looked after earlier in the day was also sitting there and he rose as she approached.

'Susi, this is Richard Fairchild.' Clive made the introduction.

'Oh!'

'It's very good to meet you, at last,' he said, smiling warmly and shaking her hand.

Susannah sat down quickly. This must be Greg's father and the head of the Fairchild Corporation! Oh, my goodness, she thought. Has he come to close us down?

'I'm so sorry I wasn't able to speak to you earlier,' she apologised. He probably thought he should have had the personal attention of the management, Susannah thought.

But he dispelled that notion immediately. 'No apology needed,' he said. 'I could see how busy you were. You've certainly had one hell of a day.'

She couldn't help smiling back at him. He was so open and friendly, his eyes twinkling. That, she realised, made him look very much like his son, at least when he was in a good mood. They had the same strong facial features, broad shoulders and that air of confidence, although sometimes in Greg it came over much more as arrogance, Susannah admitted to herself.

'No, what I meant was, I've been very remiss in not meeting you sooner,' Richard Fairchild continued.

Susannah couldn't understand what he meant. She must have looked puzzled because he laughed gently and explained, 'The Fairchild training course, Susannah. I know it's been a few years ago now, but I remember you were one of our best trainees. I was looking forward to seeing you at the farewell dinner. But I believe some emergency called you away?'

'Yes, that's right,' Susannah replied hesitantly. What had Greg told him?

140

'Well, I'm just glad you came back to the Corporation. I hear you've done a wonderful job here. Clive's been singing your praises.'

Susannah felt herself blush, something she thought she had grown out of at university. Trust Clive, she thought. But then another thought hit her. What would Greg tell his father when he arrived back? Would Fairchild senior be quite so friendly then?

As the evening wore on, it became clear that the rain was easing up. When one of the waiters went outside and announced that it had, indeed, finally stopped, there was a rousing cheer from everyone in the lounge. As the guests started departing for bed, Susannah got up from what had turned out to be a most congenial evening. She had been nervous to start with, in the company of the head of the Fairchild Corporation. She felt as though she were on trial, back on one of the decisive training course sessions, afraid to say too much in case it reflected badly on the hotel. But she soon found that he was good company, easy to talk with and fascinating to listen to, with amusing tales of his early days in business.

She excused herself to her two companions and went over to see Peter and Samuel, making arrangements for the following day: sweeping the patios, clearing the pools and taking the furniture back outside. She took the opportunity of thanking the staff who were still on duty for their extra efforts in difficult circumstances.

As she walked back towards reception, she bumped into a table, sending a glass crashing onto the floor. She bent to gather up the debris, realising how tired she was. But a moment later, she was shocked wide awake by the familiarly cutting tones of the man who had been on her mind most of the day.

'Really, Susannah. I do hope that's not because you're tipsy?'

'What?' She couldn't believe he was accusing her of drinking. A single cocktail after dinner and then soft drinks was all she ever allowed herself when she was on duty. That hadn't changed tonight.

'Oh, come on, Greg. Give the girl a break. She's been working her butt off while you've been away.' Once again Clive came to her rescue, singing her praises.

'And a superb job she's done too.' Susannah couldn't believe that Richard Fairchild was echoing Clive's words; Greg could hardly disagree with him.

'Father!'

Susannah looked at Greg. He was clearly shocked at seeing his father and, she guessed, he was probably having the same thoughts as she had earlier: was he the bearer of bad news for the hotel?

The two men shook hands, somewhat stiffly, Susannah noticed, and then, much to her embarrassment, Fairchild senior repeated his earlier comments. 'Susannah has been on the go all day long, Greg. She hasn't stopped. She's done a tremendous job keeping everyone happy in this weather while you've been away. Are you all right, my dear?'

He turned away from his son and put a solicitous hand on Susannah's arm, taking the broken glass from her hand. Clive moved forward to help him and Susannah couldn't help glancing at Greg, to see his reaction at the attention she was receiving. He looked, she saw, as exhausted as she felt.

'I'm sorry, Susannah,' he obviously felt pressurised into apologising. 'That was a bad joke at a bad time. I'm sorry.'

'That's okay, Greg,' she replied, desperate just to get away from all the undercurrents. 'I can tell you what's been happening if you'd like …'

'No way, sweetie.' Clive's endearment was just a little out of place but neither of the others seemed to notice. 'It's bedtime for you.'

'Yes, I think we could all do with a good night's sleep,' Richard Fairchild's tone brooked no argument. 'I think some R 'n R is what's called for tomorrow, for us all. Business can wait.' Without waiting for a reply, he said his goodnights and made his way to reception, accompanied by Channing.

'What is he doing here?' Greg's tone was softer now but still insistent.

'Your father? I have no idea.'

'So he hasn't told you what he intends doing with the hotel?'

'Of course not.' Susannah was indignant. As if she would discuss business with the head of the Fairchild Corporation without Greg. He obviously didn't trust her at all.

Greg sat down heavily in the nearest chair and waved his hand in Susannah's direction. 'I'm sorry,' he said. 'I'm just whacked. I don't know what I'm saying, and it was just a shock to see him here. That's all. Sorry, Susannah.'

Two apologies from Greg in one night was almost more than she could take. Susannah sat down opposite him. He did look rough, she thought.

'How was your journey back?'

'Horrendous. The road's flooded for miles and at Shimo, there's been a landslide,' he said, mentioning a village not many miles away.

'The new arrivals had a bit of a fright,' Susannah said. Normally that would have brought an instant reaction from her boss but he let it go, bending forward to rest his head in his hands.

'Some of the staff couldn't get here and some can't get back. They're staying here the night.' She thought that at least would provoke a reaction. But it didn't.

143

'Good. Good.' He looked up. 'It must have been a bad day. I'm sorry I was away. Really. I'll make it up to you, I promise.'

Greg leaned over and caught Susannah's hands in his. For a second, their eyes met. Greg rose and pulled Susannah up with him. Too tired to move, Susannah held her breath, wondering what was coming next. Surely he wasn't planning on carrying on from where they had been interrupted the night before?

'Goodnight, Miss Susannah; goodnight, Mr Greg.' Peter's voice echoed over the reception and the two of them pulled back. Susannah found the strength to walk away, echoing Peter's words over her shoulder. As she collected her key, she glanced back, and a shaft of light fell on Greg's face. She expected to see weariness and worry; what she hadn't expected was the sheer anguish etched in every line.

Chapter 26

I've lost control, Greg thought. I've completely lost control. He, who always prided himself on being the go-getter, the do-er, the leader, the man. He was no longer in charge, and he didn't like it one little bit.

What was happening to him? First it was that Eshe, ordering him to take her to the airport. He'd never promised her anything so why should she be so upset when he had put his foot down over any sort of commitment? It was she who had changed: from a sexy, fun-loving girlfriend into a clinging would-be wife. Why were women all the same? Surely some of them just wanted a bit of fun? He'd found plenty like that in the past. So where were they all now?

Then there had been all that nonsense at the airport when he had finally seen her off. She had given him a piece of her mind and none too quietly. Told him just what she thought of him. Words like shallow, vain, insincere, workaholic still echoed in his head. Her parting gibe had just been ridiculous: in love with his assistant manager. Where had that idea come from? He'd got Susannah out of his system long ago.

The day had not got any better after that. He'd had a terrible drive back from Mombasa airport through one of the worst storms in living memory for this time of the year. When he had finally walked into the hotel, completely drenched and shattered, there was his father, the man he had barely exchanged a dozen words with over the past year. Not only that, but he had been laughing and joking with Susannah and Channing. Greg couldn't remember the last time he'd seen his father laughing. Certainly not in the last five years, since John's death. No, nothing had brought a smile to his face, or a kind word to his lips. So how come he had turned up here, at the Sunset Beach, completely unannounced?

145

Then, to cap it all, Greg had been told – no, ordered – to be ready for a ten o'clock departure the following day. His father had decided that all four of them were off on safari. Greg had objected, saying, quite reasonably he thought, that the hotel shouldn't be left without both its managers. But he'd been outflanked by the others. They would only be away for two days, he was told. Many of their guests were themselves away on trips. Susannah had already briefed Peter and Rosalie on what was needed to keep the hotel running smoothly. In the case of an emergency, they would only be, at the most, two hours' drive away.

Completely hi-jacked was how Greg had felt, and a distinct lack of sleep hadn't brought any clearer thoughts come the morning.

'Good morning, Greg.' Greg's thoughts were interrupted, and he turned to find his father at his side, overnight bag in hand.

'Morning, er, Dad,' Greg greeted him awkwardly. They hadn't had a chance to make more than polite conversation the previous night. Before that, the last time they had spoken had ended in a major row, with Greg walking out, determined to make it on his own. Fairchild senior nodded.

'I'm really looking forward to this. Haven't been on a safari for twenty-five years. I would imagine they're a lot more comfortable now, eh?'

'Oh, er, yes, I'm sure they are.' Greg couldn't get used to the idea of an ordinary conversation with his father. It had always been business with them, no social chitchat and certainly no family talk.

'What? Do you mean you haven't been on one of your own safaris?'

Criticism, always criticism. Greg had grown up with the idea that he could never do well enough for his father's liking. Anything he'd done at school, if he hadn't come first, then he hadn't done his best. When he had finally joined the

146

family business, nothing he did was just right, his father always knew better.

'No, I haven't had the time. I've left that side of the business to Susannah.' He knew he sounded defensive but it was the truth after all.

'Right, I can understand that.'

Greg couldn't believe his ears. His father agreeing with him?

'So it looks as though we're both in for a treat. I've been hearing great things about Susannah's safaris and her talks. Sounds as though you have a real diamond there. Just what the Fairchild Corporation teaches, a strong management team.'

He still couldn't resist the opportunity to lecture, Greg thought. But if they were to be spending the best part of the next two days together in a jeep, Greg knew he had to compromise. He took a deep breath and, much against his inclination, agreed with his father.

'Yes, Dad, you're absolutely right. Susannah's brilliant,' to be rewarded by a look of complete astonishment on the elder Fairchild's face. Perhaps the next two days wouldn't be so bad. If things got at all tense, at least they would have Susannah and Clive as buffers.

'I don't believe you!' Channing's strangled tones sent the whole jeep into another wave of laughter, which Greg was happy to join in. The whole day had been one of the most enjoyable he could remember in many years. True, he hadn't had much of a conversation with his father as yet. The business meeting had been postponed until they got back. But everything had been more than cordial between them and he had found himself more and more relaxed, able even to recall anecdotes from his childhood and schooldays that he was happy to share with the others.

'I promise you, Clive, it really is true.' Susannah gave him a playful hug which, for some unaccountable reason, gave Greg a jolt. He and his father were sitting opposite them in the mini-van that was taking them round part of the Tsavo East Game Park. The Lodge where they were to spend the night had provided them with a substantial lunch hamper which took up most of the back seat, forcing Susannah and Clive into close proximity.

'In the 19th century, clerks or secretaries wore tailcoats and knickerbocker trousers …' Susannah's repeated explanation was drowned in an explosion of laughter from Channing. She struggled to continue, 'They had a habit of putting their quill pens behind their ears. The secretary bird, as you can see, Clive, if you weren't laughing at me so much, has twenty black crest feathers that look like quill pens behind its ears.'

'I'm not laughing at you, sweetie,' Clive took the opportunity to return Susannah's hug. 'I just cannot believe someone named a bird after a Charles Dickens' character.'

'Well, I think it fits,' Greg found himself defending his assistant manager. 'They do look just like quill pens, which, after all, were feathers, Clive, once found on a bird, you know.'

'Yes, yes, I know,' he was still laughing. 'I apologise, Susannah. I'm really not laughing at you. It's just that the name doesn't really fit with a modern secretary, does it?'

'Probably not the ones you have back home,' Greg couldn't resist the slightest of jibes but he changed the subject quickly so that no one could take offence. 'I think we should start looking for a spot for lunch, don't you. I have to say I'm famished. I never knew safaris could be quite so exhausting.'

The rest of the party was in complete agreement, having been out animal spotting for nearly four hours. Their driver, Mohammed, was the ranger who had driven Susannah and Clive on their introductory safari, and he seemed, to Greg, to know exactly where to go to each time they asked for another experience. They had already spotted elephant, antelope, ostrich, buffalo and zebra as well as a wide variety of exotic birds.

Susannah had been told that she wasn't on duty but she had been more than happy to supply the answers to Clive and Richard's endless questions about the animals and their environment. Once more Greg was impressed with her knowledge but even more so with the way she expressed it. This was no dry zoological lecture. This was a woman who knew her stuff and her audience. She was quite happy to have Clive laugh at her anecdote about the secretary bird. He would probably remember that titbit of information for the rest of his life.

'Did you ever think of going into teaching?' Greg looked up sharply. His father had just asked Susannah the very question he had been pondering. She would make an excellent teacher, he realised. She had a good speaking voice, knew her subject thoroughly, could communicate it to all sorts of audiences and, he remembered from the training course, had well overcome her shyness at being the centre of attention.

They had stopped the minivan in the shade of a stand of acacia trees in the middle of a great plain with hardly another tree in sight, let alone anything else. Mohammed had assured them that they would be quite safe getting out of the jeep: rule number one for all safaris was that no one got out of the jeep, or even put their head out of the window, unless the driver or ranger allowed it. Wild animals could appear literally from nowhere extremely quickly.

But Mohammed said this was a safe spot. He arranged the canvas chairs and unpacked their lunch and was now standing some ten metres away with a gun hanging loosely at his side. He'd never had to use one in the fifteen years he'd been employed by the Lodge, but he would never take any chances.

149

'Teaching? I did the one-year course at university and quite enjoyed the teaching practice, but I never thought of a teaching job when I left. I think I enjoy being out here too much. Classrooms would be too confining!' Susannah smiled warmly at the elder Fairchild, her response totally natural. Greg watched as she chatted to the others. She was right: this was her environment. This was where she shone, where she belonged. He noticed that her hair had lightened over the past few months, becoming a warm, attractive honey blonde while the colour of her skin had deepened into an attractive golden glow.

'Don't you agree, Greg?' Caught unawares, Greg just couldn't respond to Channing's query.

'Sorry, miles away,' he confessed, realising it was the furthest it could be from the truth.

'I don't blame you,' his father smiled over at him. 'I bet this is the first time in ages that you've been away from the hotel to relax.'

Unbidden, Greg's thoughts went immediately to the evening at the Majestic that he had spent with Susannah. He'd certainly not been working that time. He couldn't help but glance at her and noticed, with some perverse satisfaction, that she was looking down, staring intently at her sandwich. He felt sure she was remembering too.

'Miss Susannah?' The luncheon party was suddenly interrupted by the anxious tones of Mohammed. He was pointing into the distance. Susannah spoke to him in Swahili and turned to the others with a worried look on her face.

'He's saying that the weather's changing. He's quite concerned. He thinks we ought to get to the Lodge as soon as possible.'

Chapter 27

An hour later and they knew they had left just in time. They had driven to the lodge under steadily darkening skies and within minutes of their arrival, the storm had broken and what a storm it was turning out to be! Even Mohammed said he'd never seen anything like it. The manager greeted Susannah and Clive like long-lost friends and was equally welcoming to Greg and his father. Their luggage was dispatched to their rooms while they were invited to recover from their somewhat hectic drive with tea, coffee, pastries and anything stronger they wanted.

At first Greg thought all the attention was because of his father, the head of the Fairchild Corporation. But he soon realised that the staff at the Lodge were equally considerate to all the guests who had been forced inside on such a day. He also found himself impressed by the Lodge itself. As his father had rightly guessed, it was a considerable improvement on the facilities they had experienced on the couple of safaris they had taken as a family when he and John were young.

'Well, I suggest we all have a rest and meet back at dusk,' Channing's voice broke into Greg's study of his surroundings. Clive was saying what everyone was thinking, Greg realised.

'What a good idea,' he said, his words echoed by his father. They turned and smiled at each other, giving Greg a strange feeling; he hadn't seen that look directed at himself for a long time. But as he held his father's gaze, he realised that he was looking old. Close up, Greg could see the lines etched in his father's face, the grey in his hair that he was sure hadn't been there the last time the two had met.

Susannah broke the moment with a sigh as Channing helped her to her feet. He was always there, Greg thought with annoyance. Always at Susannah's side, attending to her every

151

need. No wonder she hadn't had any time for him. Channing had insinuated himself well and truly into Susannah's affections.

Thoroughly refreshed after a shower and half an hour's catnap, Greg wandered back into the lounge. He had been surprised to find that his shirt and slacks had not only been unpacked from his overnight bag, but they had been ironed and laid out for him. What service! It was amazing that anyone returned to the Sunset Beach after a safari like this.

Now he found that service extended all across the Lodge. He was greeted personally by a waiter and told that Miss Susannah was down at the hide. When he looked quizzical, the waiter showed him to the walkway and accompanied him down to the semi-underground hide. Susannah was there, binoculars in hand, engrossed in watching a group of baboons who had braved the still pouring rain to visit the watering-hole. She jumped when the waiter asked if they would like drinks.

'I'll have a fruit cocktail,' Greg replied. 'Susannah?'

'The same, please, Michael.' Once again Greg was impressed at the very natural way in which she responded to the waiter; not many people bothered to find out the names of the hired hands. His first thought was to wonder if it was really necessary, but on seeing the waiter's smile, he recognised it was.

'Did you have a good rest?' Susannah turned back to the viewing window. The animals were so close that Greg felt he could have put out his hand and touched them. He moved closer and was annoyed to see Susannah back away from him. He was about to say something when a group of other guests came down the walkway. To allow them good access to the window, he and Susannah had to move away and closer to each other.

'Isn't this fantastic?' Anyone would think this was her first visit, Greg thought. But her enthusiasm was certainly catching as she started to explain to him about yellow baboons. She was speaking quietly, for his ears only, but the other guests gradually fell silent and listened in. Greg fully expected Susannah to stop, even to blush as she had done on many occasions when she had found herself the centre of attention on the training course. But this was a different Susannah, a more confident young woman. She responded to the interest and, without in any way showing off, gave them the benefit of her expertise. Another guest joined them.

'Oh, excuse me, are you Susannah?'

In response to her nod, the woman continued. 'Your husband said he'd be right along and that he's got the drinks.'

'Oh, he's not my husband,' Susannah was quick to put the woman right.

'Oh, I'm sorry,' she said, turning to Greg. 'My apologies. Silly me.'

Greg could sense that Susannah was about to put the woman right a second time but he was saved from any sort of intervention by Channing's arrival, complete with drinks.

The next half-hour proved something of a trial for Greg. With the other guests disappearing to the restaurant, the three of them had the hide to themselves and they were treated to an ever-changing vista of animals, large and small, right in front of them. Susannah added her expertise from time to time. But what annoyed Greg was the proprietorial way in which Channing treated Susannah. He was forever putting his arm round her shoulders to direct her attention to another visitor to the water-hole. Or he was offering to hold her drink for her while she used the binoculars. He laughed at her comments, praised her knowledge and even smoothed her hair back from her face, unasked.

Greg found it hard not to say something. If they were becoming that friendly, he reckoned, that was fine. But there was no need to flaunt it in front of him. To be fair, he thought, Susannah wasn't responding in kind. She was, if anything, dividing her attention equally between the two of them, answering their queries, pointing out the animals, sharing in jokes and anecdotes.

But Greg knew his temper was rising and that the others weren't that wrapped up in each other not to notice.

'Are you all right, Greg?' Susannah sounded concerned.

Greg cringed.

'Safari too much for you? You've gone very quiet.'

'I'm … er … just wondering where my father has got to.' He came up with a suitable excuse at the last second. 'He was quite tired from the journey,'

Susannah spoke sympathetically. 'I expect he's had a good rest. I suggested we meet around eight for dinner, so perhaps we should go back to the Lodge?'

Channing took that as another opportunity to guide Susannah back along the walkway, Greg bringing up the rear. As they reached the Lodge, Greg spotted his father, sitting in one of the comfortable armchairs, sipping at a drink. Susannah was right, he thought. His father did look tired. Perhaps the storm would prove to be a blessing. He wouldn't have enjoyed another couple of hours out in the jeep. Greg made a mental note to make sure they didn't keep him up too late. They could all do with a proper night's sleep.

Chapter 28

The next morning, it was clear that at least two of the party hadn't had a comfortable night at all. As Greg approached the breakfast table, he could see immediately that his father was still looking tired. So too was Susannah. 'I'm a very light sleeper,' she was explaining. 'I just couldn't block out the noise of the wind and rain.'

'Me, too,' Greg heard his father reply. 'But I don't want to spoil the party. I'll be all right in the minivan.'

Once Greg and Channing joined them, the talk turned to the day's planned drives. But as Clive began enthusing about a pride of lions that had been sighted some distance away, Greg knew he had to intervene.

'Actually, Clive,' he interrupted. 'I think we should take it a bit easy today. I know I didn't get much sleep in the storm and Susannah and I need to firm up things with the manager. We're about to bring a lot of business his way and I want to make sure that everything's right.'

Out of the corner of his eye, he caught a glance of annoyance on Susannah's face. Oh, God, he thought. I've put my foot in it. She'll think that I'm checking up on her. She's probably got everything sorted.

But she surprised him by agreeing. 'I think you're right, Greg,' she said. 'We'll make it a short tour this morning, come back, have lunch here and take it easy for the rest of the day. If anyone wants to go out again, then they can. Mohammed and the minivan are at our disposal all day. But I know I'd like to catch up on my sleep.'

Greg shot her a look that tried to say sorry and thank you in one go and he was relieved when she smiled back at him, nodding ever so slightly in his father's direction. As they broke up to get ready for the morning drive, Greg caught Susannah by the arm.

'Thank you,' he said.

'No problem,' she replied. 'I was going to suggest we had a quieter day. Clive gets quite carried away sometimes and neither your father nor I had a particularly good night. It was good that you put your foot down.'

'And that's probably the only time I'll ever hear you say that!' Greg responded with a smile, relieved again when Susannah grinned back at him.

'Too right!'

The atmosphere in the jeep wasn't anything near as lively as the day before. Today it more than matched the dark skies that had appeared within minutes of their departure. Even Channing was subdued, making only half-hearted attempts at his usual banter. When the rain started, no one raised any objections to Mohammed's suggestion that they return to the Lodge for an early lunch.

But as they turned round and started back, the sky was rent by forks of lightening, accompanied by cracks of thunder and a ten-fold increase in the rain. The shallow river they had crossed on their way out was now feet deep and Mohammed braked hard when he saw it.

'I dare not take the van through that, Miss Susannah,' he said. 'We will have to go back the longer route. But I think it will be safer.'

The party agreed and once again Mohammed turned the minivan around. The roads in Tsavo East were usually in a good state, particularly as the park actively discouraged off-roading. But after 36 hours of almost constant rain, it was becoming clearer by the minute that many of the roads had literally been washed away. Their progress was constantly hampered by the effects of the rain, pools of water that could have been an inch deep, or two feet, had to be avoided and twice Greg and Clive had to brave the elements to push the van out of the mud.

They had just got going again after a particularly bad patch when Greg looked over at his father. He had gone quite grey, Greg realised, and hadn't spoken for quite a while.

'Dad, are you …' Greg's words were lost as the van hit a series of ruts. Mohammed fought to correct the steering but just as everyone thought he had succeeded, the front tyres hit another obstruction and the van was thrown sideways, tilted, and landed with a sickening thud at an angle.

Even though the four passengers had all been wearing seat belts, Greg and Channing found themselves almost on top of his father and Susannah who were pinioned against the window, now inches deep in mud. Greg could see that Channing was moving, trying to undo the seat belt that held him, but the other two were motionless.

'Dad, Susannah … are you are right?'

He yanked at his own seat belt which came away easily, clearly damaged in the accident, and he only just stopped himself from falling even more heavily on Susannah.

'Oh!'

'Susannah, thank God. Are you all right?'

Greg worked his body into a position where she had more room and gently helped her untangle her limbs from the awkward position she had fallen into. He glanced round and saw that Clive was doing the same for his father.

'My arm hurts,' Susannah's voice wavered. 'But I think I'm all right otherwise.'

'Greg,' Channing's voice was sharp and Greg turned round quickly.

'What is it?'

'Your Dad. I think he's been knocked unconscious. Can we get him into a better position?'

A low moan came from the front of the van. Susannah heaved herself up into a sitting position and looked over the back of her seat.

'I'll help Mohammed,' she said, motioning Greg to assist Channing. It took some time for the two younger men to get Richard Fairchild out of the corner of the vehicle. A gash on the side of his head confirmed Channing's initial opinion, for the older man was still not moving.

'If you hold him, I'll see if I can get the jeep upright,' Greg suggested, crawling out of the opposite window and falling, with a squelch, into the mud below. He went round the front and looked in through the shattered windscreen, to see Susannah supporting Mohammed. There was no mistaking his broken leg.

'I can help, bwana,' he was saying but Greg just shook his head and went round to the side now buried in the mud.

'Susannah, can you move Mohammed over to the other side? It might adjust the balance,' he said.

Slowly, and with a great deal of effort, Greg gradually inched the van into a more upright position, its wheels sinking more and more into the oozing red mud. With Channing's help, Greg moved his father into the recovery position and was much relieved when he saw his eyelids eventually flicker open.

'Don't speak, Dad,' Greg urged. His father's breathing was laboured as he tried desperately to say something. His hand fluttered weakly and his breath came out in gasps.

'He's pointing to his pocket,' Susannah suddenly said, having returned to the back of the van to get the first aid kit.

'Dad, Dad what is it?' Greg bent low towards his father and could just make out the words 'My pills.'

Greg felt into his father's jacket and located a vial. He unscrewed the lid and tipped some out onto his palm. They were small and pale pink.

'They're for angina,' Susannah said, looking at the vial. 'Put one under his tongue, Greg. It'll ease the pain.'

Greg did so and after a while his father was able to sit up. Greg had never seen him look so grey or so old. He took off his own jacket and put it round his father's shoulders.

'Greg, can you come here and see Mohammed, please.' Susannah called from the front seat where she had fashioned a makeshift splint for their driver's leg. He went round to the offside door and peered in. Susannah put her finger to her lips.

'I think we should get your father to hospital as quickly as possible,' she whispered. 'Can you get the van out of here?'

Greg raised his hands in a helpless gesture and was startled when Susannah grabbed him by the shoulder and shook him.

'Greg, your father could be having a heart attack. There's no point in trying to make it back to the Lodge. Our best bet is to head for Mombasa. The hospital is on this side of the city, Mohammed says. It could take less than an hour. What do you think?'

'I don't even know if the van will run,' Greg replied, lowering his voice to match hers. 'We've got to get it out of this mud, first.'

'There are boards in the back, under the seat,' Mohammed volunteered. 'We often have to use them. It should be okay.'

Susannah helped Mohammed move into the back, where he could rest his injured leg, letting Channing into the driver's seat. It took thirty precious minutes to get the van back into action, Greg working tirelessly at the wheels, positioning and repositioning the boards until the tyres finally got a grip.

'Ok, now to see if the engine holds up,' he said and flung himself into the passenger seat, next to Clive.

'Hey, I can't drive this thing,' Channing protested. 'That's up to you!'

'No, no, you'll do fine,' came Greg's sharp retort. 'I'll navigate.'

Channing reluctantly turned the engine over and despite an unnatural whine the minivan began to move forward. But after barely a few yards, he stamped on the brakes.

'Greg, I can't do this. I don't drive. I have no idea what I'm doing. I'm more of a liability,' Channing's voice was rising.

Greg sat stock still, not saying a word. He stared out in front of him, at the rain. His eyes glazed over. He was remembering that day when John had taken his place in the rally. It had been a day like this, monsoon weather. John had never been so confident.

'Hey, bruv. This is old hat to you and me. See you at the finish. Have the champagne ready!'

'Greg! Greg!' He felt hands pull at his shirt and for a split second it was that nightmare all over again: people calling to him, holding him back, forcing him to do nothing but watch as the car burst into flames.

'Greg!'

It was the scream that woke him out of his trance and he turned to see Susannah's face inches from his own. He felt a sting on his cheek. She had slapped him!

'You've got to drive, Greg. You've just got to.'

Chapter 29

'Please, please, can you tell me how they are? Are they all right? Is my father conscious? Anything, please, tell me.'

From the other side of the cubicle curtain, Susannah could hear Greg's entreaties. She tried to raise herself up but was hampered by the cast that had been put on her arm. She lay back and tried to call out, but it was too late; she heard Greg being ushered away by the nurse, saying they would fetch him as soon as the doctors had finished.

'Nurse?'

This time her words got through and the nurse came in.

'Are you okay, my dear?'

'Yes, yes, I'm fine, thank you. I just wanted to know about Mr Fairchild. How is he?'

'He's just a tad impatient, isn't he? Typical man.'

The nurse smiled knowingly.

'What?' Susannah was totally confused. Had she suffered concussion too? 'No, no, sorry. Not that Mr Fairchild. He's always like that. I meant Richard, Mr Fairchild senior. How is he?'

'Oh, he's not doing too badly. The doctors have settled him down. He's just down the corridor. No, miss, you can't ….'

She broke off as Susannah tried to get off the bed, struggling with her arm. 'Look, I'll help you into a wheelchair and then I'll take you down to him. You've both been through quite an ordeal, and we'd like to keep an eye on you overnight. You can keep him company until we have beds in the ward for you all. But we don't want him upset. That other Mr Fairchild will just have to wait.'

Susannah was so relieved to see the colour back in Richard's face that she pushed herself out of the wheelchair

161

before the nurse could stop her and leant over to give him a kiss on the cheek. His eyes opened and for a split second, she thought she was looking at Greg. The family likeness was all too apparent.

'Oh, my dear, that's so sweet of you. It's a long time since I was kissed by a lovely lady.'

Susannah blushed as Richard patted her hand, the Fairchild charm very much in evidence.

'You're looking so much better,' she said softly. 'We were quite worried.'

'I know and I'm sorry to have put everyone to such trouble,' came the considerate reply. 'I didn't want Greg to know about the angina, and until last night, it was well under control.'

'How are you now?'

'I'm feeling better. A day or so here, the doctor says, and I should be fine. I guess I'll be needing a holiday somewhere nice.'

The smile was all Fairchild, Susannah decided. 'What about you? Your arm?'

Susannah explained that she'd suffered a fractured radius and that, because she wasn't sure whether she'd been knocked out or just fainted in the crash, they wanted to keep an eye on her too.

'And the others?'

'Greg and Clive have cuts and bruises,' Susannah replied. 'I think they're both exhausted too and Mohammed's leg should mend all right, they've said.'

'You did well, young lady,' Richard complimented her. 'Looking after us all.'

'I did nothing,' Susannah replied. 'I think Greg did the most.'

'Yes, he got us out of the mud. Strong bones, we Fairchilds have.' The neutral tone in which the elder Fairchild dismissed his son's efforts struck a chord in Susannah.

162

She took a deep breath. 'No, it's not just that,' she said. 'Driving us back, that took a lot of guts.'

'Well, I agree it was bad storm …' Richard Fairchild started but Susannah cut him short.

'It's not that, Richard, and I think you know it,' she said softly, moving closer to the bed. 'It's the memories and the guilt. For a while it looked as though he wasn't going to get through those.'

There was a moment's silence. Fairchild senior stared fixedly at the wall but then brought his gaze back to meet Susannah's.

'You'd better tell me exactly what you mean, young lady,' he said.

The next day Susannah was back at the Sunset Beach with a clean bill of health but with instructions to take things easy. Richard Fairchild had been kept in a little longer for a full check-up, but the doctors were pleased with his progress too and Greg had just left to pick him up.

Susannah smiled as she remembered the expression on Greg's face when his father had turned down his offer of a flight to take him straight back to his home in Paris.

'No, thank you,' came the reply. 'I want a holiday. And I want it right here in Kenya. Do you happen to know a good hotel that would put up with me?'

His twinkling eyes were just like his son's, Susannah recalled. It would be good to have him around. They had had several long talks while they were in the hospital. She had learned a lot about Greg's family life, from his mother dying when he and John were just young teens, to John's accident six years ago. Richard had admitted to her that, without his wife to contribute a mother's influence, he had been strict on both boys. Too strict, he realised now.

'I could never talk to Greg,' he had confided. 'He always seemed to be holding himself apart, particularly from

163

me. I knew he got on well with his brother, despite their age difference. I think I was envious.'

Susannah had hesitated before saying anything, aware that she was party to the other side of the story. But, in the end, she couldn't hold back. 'Greg thinks you blame him.'

'Blame him? For what?'

'For John's death. For encouraging him to take up rally driving and for letting him drive on that last rally.'

The look on Richard's face had sent Susannah into a panic. He had gone quite grey again, as grey as on the ill-fated safari and she had pressed the bell to summon the nurse. When she returned to see him later, it was she who felt guilty at having worried him so. But he brushed aside her apologies, saying that she had done him a favour and now was the time for some plain speaking.

The sympathy and support hadn't been all one way. Reluctant at first, Susannah had finally opened up and told the head of the Fairchild Corporation that she had left the training scheme when her father was shot by ivory poachers. Fairchild was upset that he hadn't been informed of the real reason she had left.

'There were a lot of rumours flying around,' he told her, but he hadn't elaborated, looking almost embarrassed in talking about it.

Susannah thought she could guess what the rumours had been about. Herself and Greg, no doubt. When she told him how she had come to be at the Sunset Beach, he couldn't have been any nicer, she recalled. In talking about her father, she hadn't been able to hold back the tears and Richard had offered a friendly shoulder for her to cry on.

So, Susannah thought, here she was, lounging in her quiet corner of the hotel grounds with a swing seat that had been set up for her as a surprise by the staff, a table loaded with drinks and fruit, strict instructions not to worry about anything to do with work and a pile of paperbacks that she had never had time to read. If that wasn't enough, she had at her beck and call the personal service of one Clive Channing.

He had been extremely subdued once they had made it back to Mombasa. At first Susannah thought it was the effect of the crash and even voiced her concerns to the doctors. But physically he was pronounced to be in good shape. It was only later, back at the hotel, that he confided to Susannah that he was embarrassed.

'What?' Susannah had no idea what he was talking about.

'I was useless, Susi,' he said. 'I couldn't help at all in the crisis.'

'Oh, Clive, that's nonsense,' Susannah couldn't help smiling sympathetically at his crestfallen expression. 'You helped Greg get the car sorted. You looked after Richard. You got us back to Mombasa. You were brilliant.'

He cheered up at Susannah's words but had another confession. 'I've never learnt to drive, you see, Susi. I've never really needed to.'

'There's no need to apologise, Clive.' Susannah realised now what he meant. 'Greg didn't know that. He shouldn't have presumed. It really doesn't matter.'

'But I put Greg in an awkward position,' Clive persisted.

'Actually, I think you did him a favour,' Susannah said. 'Has he told you about his brother?'

'Yes, a little. I got the impression he felt responsible.'

'Yes,' Susannah agreed. 'I think he's finally come to terms with the fact that his brother led his own life and that Greg couldn't be responsible for his actions. Anyway, let's talk about something nicer. Are you off to Nairobi?'

Once again Clive looked embarrassed. 'Actually, Susi, I'm off back home. That's what I've come to tell you.'

'What? I thought you still had business to attend to.' Susannah knew she was going to miss the burly American.

'Oh, I have. But now is not the time to talk to Richard or Greg, I think. So, I'm going back home but I want to book in now for next year.'

'No problem,' Susannah replied with a smile and a hug, although she couldn't help wondering whether she would actually be here to greet him again. Things hadn't exactly come to a head between her and Greg, but they certainly weren't comfortable either.

'But I've something to ask you, Susi.'

She dragged her thoughts back to the present. Surely Clive couldn't be on the verge of …. no, please, she thought desperately. She knew he had become fond of her over the past couple of months, but she had never given him any more encouragement other than friendship.

'Susi, I was wondering, no hoping, that you might think about coming to work for me,' Clive said, looking anxiously at her. 'I mean I know you love it out here. But if anything happens to make you change your mind, well, then I think you'd be the perfect manager for any number of my concerns back home. Would you think about it?'

'Oh, Clive, I don't know what to say.'

'You don't have to say anything now, Susi, my dear,' Clive leant forward to kiss her on the cheek. 'Perhaps it's come a bit out of the blue. But you know what I think of you. Promise me you'll consider it?'

Susannah could only nod, her mind in a whirl. America? Might that be the answer? To get away completely from the man she had fallen in love with five years ago but who clearly didn't want any sort of permanent relationship? Perhaps there were too many memories here and a change of scene was just what she needed to get on with the rest of her life.

'So, if you fancy a holiday in Boston, just say the word and I'll arrange it,' Clive was clearly back to normal as

166

he prepared to leave the hotel. Greg had brought his father back earlier and Clive had said his farewells to them. Now, he was taking his leave of Susannah, and she too was in a very positive mood.

'That's a lovely idea, Clive,' she said, helping to stack his cases in the taxi. 'I've never been there and it would be a lovely break.'

'Oh, Susi, I'm going to miss you,' Clive reached out and enveloped her in a big hug, kissing her warmly on the cheek. 'Take care of yourself, honey.'

'I will, Clive,' Susannah felt quite sad. He had been a good friend during quite a trying time, and she wasn't sure how the next few months would turn out without him around. 'I'll see you in Boston,' she promised, returning his kiss.

Chapter 30

'I'll see you in Boston.'

Greg knew he was spying but he just couldn't help himself. He leaned further out of the window and could barely suppress a gasp when he saw the two of them exchange a kiss and a warm embrace. So, she was going to join him in the States. He realised he wasn't that surprised, and he really couldn't blame her, considering everything that had happened over the last few months.

But even setting all logic aside, Greg found that he was incredibly upset. Susannah had awoken feelings in him that he had thought were dead and buried forever. He had found out that those feelings weren't for women in general; they were very specifically still for her, the woman who had betrayed him those five years ago.

'Mr Greg, are you there?' Rosalie's voice intruded on Greg's thoughts, and he moved quickly away from the window.

'What is it?' He knew his tone was brusque but this time he couldn't summon the energy to do anything about it.

'There's a party arriving from the airport in half an hour. Will you greet them? Only I didn't want to ask Miss Susannah …'

'Of course not!' Greg's temper flared as he turned to face his secretary.

'Oh!'

Surely she wasn't going to burst into tears? Greg thought all that was a thing of the past; she had really improved in the last few weeks.

'What?'

'Well, who should greet them, then?'

'I shall, Rosalie. That's what I said. Susannah is not working. You know that.'

Rosalie turned and walked back out of the door, her shoulders slumped. Oh, God, Greg thought. He'd have to go and apologise. He shouldn't have raised his voice. He quickly followed her out of the office but she was nowhere to be seen. Probably in tears in the ladies, he reckoned.

He was about to turn back when he saw Susannah returning to the hotel, having seen Channing off on his trip home. In a way he had been sorry to hear that the American was leaving; they'd got on well, the two of them, and he'd certainly given Greg a few business tips. But then, Greg smiled, ruefully, Channing and Susannah had also got on well, exceptionally well if she was going to be joining him in Boston.

Greg saw that Susannah was looking extremely forlorn. Not missing him already, surely, he muttered to himself. He was about to turn away when he heard her cry out. A group of guests had been hurrying through reception and one had accidentally jogged her arm, her broken arm. The man was apologising profusely as Greg joined them.

'It's alright, Mr Harper, really. I'm all right,' Susannah reassured him. Even in the midst of a painful incident, she could recall the guest's name, Greg noticed. Nothing ever than professional, his assistant manager.

'It's all right, sir,' Greg intervened. 'I'll take care of her. You'd best get your taxi.'

Much relieved, the man rejoined his party while Greg put an arm round Susannah's shoulders and guided her gently back to the office.

'Here, sit down,' he said, moving a chair for her. 'Are you okay? Would you like a drink?' He knelt down in front of her and waited until she lifted her head. Her eyes were watery. For a moment Greg thought he was about to have another tearful female on his hands. But then Susannah's mouth curved into a smile.

'I can't believe how the smallest of movements makes it hurt.' Greg stood up hurriedly, his sympathetic demeanour was clearly superfluous.

'You really shouldn't be out in the public areas while your arm's mending, Susannah,' he couldn't keep the irritation out of his voice.

'Oh, sorry, Greg. I thought it would help if I did what I could. You know, talk to the guests and the staff. I can't get back on the computer yet but it shouldn't be long …'

Her consideration was getting under his skin. He couldn't stand it anymore.

'When will you be leaving, then?' he interrupted, forcing disinterested neutrality into his voice.

'Leaving?' She sounded completely taken aback.

'Yes, leaving. I gather you've finally achieved your aim: a rich, no, a very rich man who's totally enthralled by you. Congratulations, Susannah. It didn't work five years ago but I have to hand it to you. You've succeeded this time. I believe the Channing fortune is even larger than the Fairchild one!'

'What?'

Greg refused to turn round at the strangled exclamation from his assistant manager. He didn't want to watch her play-acting any more. In fact, the sooner she left the better.

'So, as soon as you can travel, I'm happy to let you go. Don't worry – I'll pay your sick leave and notice period. You won't be out of pocket.'

He laughed ironically; she wouldn't be worrying about money now.

'Greg, I have no idea what you're talking about.' Susannah had risen and had put her good hand on his arm. Roughly, he shook her off. No womanly wiles were going to get the better of him this time.

'We don't have to spell it out, do we, Susannah? Clive's a nice bloke, he's made his choice and you've clearly made yours. I hope you'll both be happy in Boston.'

The neutrality gave way to bitterness and Greg moved towards the door. He had to get away before his temper really got the better of him.

'Greg!' This time it wasn't a query. Susannah was actually shouting at him. He turned round to be faced by an angry young woman, her cheeks getting redder by the second. Well, she had it coming. He was going to tell her exactly what he thought.

'Hey, Greg! Do you have time for a drink? I've just been speaking to head office and they reckon they want me back. What do you think?' As Richard Fairchild walked into the office, the broad smile on his face faded instantly. 'What's going on?'

'Nothing.' Susannah and Greg answered simultaneously. Susannah held her broken arm protectively and inched past her boss.

'Excuse me, please,' she said, tight-lipped. 'I think I've overdone it today. I need to rest.'

Richard pushed the door open for her and opened his mouth to speak. But Greg forestalled him.

'Let me know your plans, then,' he said, adding sarcastically, 'When you're ready.'

Well, that was it, then, Susannah thought as she slumped down onto her bed. There really wasn't anything here for her anymore. Greg had made it quite clear that he still thought of her as a gold-digger and one that had landed a major pot of gold. Even if she explained, it wasn't going to alter his opinion of her. There was no way she could work with him any longer.

When they had been getting on, it had been possible to keep their personal history as exactly that, in the past. For a moment on that night at the Majestic, she had thought that he had started to care for her, really care, not just another conquest. But how wrong could she be?

'I'm just a hopeless judge of character,' Susannah decided. She felt like crying but knew that she would just be giving in. The accident on safari was obviously still taking its toll and she wasn't in a stable state, physically or emotionally.

Even so, she knew she had to act, before Greg had any more say in the matter. She got up and went over to the desk, getting out her address book. She would ring her old zoology professor. He had been such a support after her father had died. Susannah let out a small ironic laugh. So supportive in fact, she realised, that he had got her this job at the Sunset Beach. Look where that had led. But she felt sure he would understand her predicament now. She would explain that she and the new manager just weren't hitting it off and that she needed a new job.

She sat down and reached for the phone. She wanted this situation sorted and the sooner the better.

'This is a little beneath you, isn't it, Greg? I would have thought the luxury Fairchild resorts in Montevideo or Pattaya would be much more your style, mate!'

The strident Australian tones of Jamie Dixon echoed across the empty reception hall. Greg had been looking forward to seeing him, more than happy when Jamie had got in touch about a week's convalescence at the Sunset Beach. But his immediate reaction was to bristle at the youngster's tone.

After a moment's reflection though, he realised that to the Aussie, this must look like some second-rate Fairchild hotel. But Greg found that it didn't bother him what Jamie Dixon thought. He was proud of what he had achieved here in the last few months. This hotel was definitely on the way up. Okay, so it didn't compare to the smart resorts that he used to frequent in his globe-trotting days. But this was his, saved from closure and fast coming up to the Fairchild standard.

'Suits me, Jamie,' was his answer. He was about to explain his thinking but then stopped. Jamie wouldn't understand. Greg knew that Jamie had done well in the Corporation since their training course days. He had worked at quite a few of their hotels, gaining experience all over the world, and the talk was that he was itching for a general manager's job. Greg thought it was about time. In fact, he was quite surprised he hadn't reached that position already.

'So what about you?' was what he said instead. 'Any thoughts of where you'd like to go next?'

'What?'

Greg was surprised at the sharpness of Jamie's tone. 'Which of the Corporation's hotels you'd fancy managing?'

'Oh, oh, right,' Jamie sounded relieved at Greg's explanation. 'Anywhere will do me, mate. Not fussed at all.'

Greg wasn't taken with Jamie's laid-back manner, and he decided to cut short the tour of the Sunset Beach he had suggested when Jamie arrived. He'd probably prefer a drink in the bar, Greg thought. With any luck he could slip away and address his most recent problem, Susannah.

'Hey, Greg, who's that over there? That gorgeous Sheila in the blue dress? Looks a bit like that sweet young thing on our training course. Remember her? Sue, wasn't it? No, I remember now, Susannah. Took a shine to me, she did.'

Greg turned round to face Jamie, trying not to let the astonishment show on his face. Susannah fancying Jamie Dixon? Never in a million years. He could clearly remember conversations he and Susannah had had about Jamie's lack of success with any girl on the course, despite his persistence. Anyway, it had been Jamie who had told him about Susannah's deception.

'Good job you didn't get involved with her, then,' Greg replied, guiding Jamie away from where he had glimpsed the very woman they were talking about.

'Why, what do you mean?'

'You told me that she knew who I was all the time and that she'd made a beeline for me, just for the Fairchild fortune.'

'Not true, mate,' Jamie replied offhandedly. 'That sweet young thing didn't have it in her to deceive anyone. No, Greg old mate, that was that Yank on our course. What was her name now? Oh, yeah, Robyn. She was the one who found out who you were and was telling everyone just how much you were worth. Hey!'

Jamie let out a yelp as he suddenly found his arm in a vice-like grip.

'What the hell are you talking about, Dixon?'

'Hey, Greg, lighten up, mate. They were just two Sheilas, a long time ago. Lot of water's passed under that bridge since.'

He laughed coarsely and Greg had to resist the very strong urge to punch him. But that feeling was quickly replaced by another: total and utter remorse. On Jamie Dixon's say-so, he had really believed that Susannah was a golddigger and he had accused her of it when she came to the Sunset Beach, not once but several times over, the most recent being barely an hour ago.

He had never let her explain her sudden departure from the training course and he had nursed such resentment over the past five years that he had kept all other women well and truly at bay, believing they were only attracted to his name and wealth, things that Susannah had clearly never desired. He had to put the matter right, before she flew off to Boston.

Chapter 31

'Susannah. Would you care to join me for afternoon tea?'

Susannah stopped in her tracks as she crossed the pool patio. Quite a few guests were enjoying the late afternoon sun and at first she wasn't sure who had called out to her. Since the accident, everyone had been incredibly caring and sympathetic, so much so that she found she couldn't be seen in the hotel's public areas without being stopped a dozen times by well-meaning well-wishers.

She really didn't want that right now. She just wanted to tell Greg Fairchild that she had another job lined up. Well, not a hundred per cent lined up, she admitted to herself. But her old zoology tutor had again come up trumps. He knew of a school in South Africa that was looking for a science tutor, with a speciality in zoology, and he would recommend her immediately.

Problem sorted, Susannah thought. A huge part of her didn't want to leave the Sunset Beach at all. But circumstances had conspired against her, and this was the ideal opportunity of getting away that she just couldn't pass up. If that didn't work out, she always had Clive's offer to consider. But now, she was going to ask Greg for a reference: he couldn't deny her that, surely?

'Susannah?' She recognised the voice now: it was Richard Fairchild and for a moment, Susannah felt guilty. Here she was, leaving the Fairchild Corporation for a second time. The man would think she had no staying power.

'Richard, I'd be delighted.' She really couldn't turn him down. They had become friends in the short time they had known each other, and he was going back home to Paris the next day.

He reminded her very much of her own father. Both were easy to talk to, easy to listen to, caring men. What a shame he and Greg didn't get on better. They ordered tea and chatted easily about the hotel until Richard paused and said,

'So, do you know Jamie Dixon?'

Susannah's head jerked upright at the unexpected question. Why should he be asking her that? 'Yes, we were on the same training course,' she replied hesitatingly.

'Oh, right, yes, I remember now,' Richard replied. There was a pause. 'He's here, you know.'

'What?' Susannah nearly dropped her cup. 'I saw him just now. Greg's taking him on a tour of the hotel. I believe he was one of the candidates for your job.'

I bet he was, thought Susannah. Now he's arrived at just the right moment. Greg will have his wish at last: me gone and his mate installed.

'Susannah?'

She realised she had been staring into the distance and that she had been clenching her jaw. She forced herself to relax and look at Richard. 'Yes?'

'From your expression, I would guess that you don't like him?'

Susannah hesitated again. She could hardly criticise a fellow employee to the head of the Fairchild Corporation.

'You are too loyal, Susannah. Don't think I don't appreciate that,' Richard said, leaning over to pat her arm. 'But I've already made my mind up about Dixon and I'm afraid that I'll have to tell Greg. He's been out of the loop too long and doesn't know what Dixon's been up to.'

'Up to?' Susannah echoed his words.

'Yes. Up to no good, it seems, wherever he's been. He was quite a promising trainee, five years ago,' Richard explained. 'But then head office started getting reports back that his personal life was beginning to intrude on his work life.'

Susannah nodded, remembering how he had come on to her several times during their course, the last occasion most forcefully in a locked room, when he had told her about Greg.

'So you do know what I'm talking about?'

Richard had clearly seen Susannah's reaction.

'I think so,' she replied. 'He was just full of himself and thought all the girls should be too.'

'Yes, that's been his downfall,' Richard agreed. 'Female staff in nearly all the hotels he's ever worked in have complained about varying degrees of harassment. And he was sent back to Paris from our Japanese venture just two weeks ago when a guest complained.'

'So what's he doing here?'

'I guess he's come to butter up Greg into giving him a job,' he said. 'But I'm going to make sure that doesn't happen. Greg's got the best assistant manager he could possibly have, Susannah, and Jamie Dixon is on his way out of the Fairchild Corporation.'

'Susannah?'

'Greg?'

The pool patio was deserted as guests were getting ready for dinner. Susannah, having failed to find Greg earlier, had wandered out of her room for what she reckoned would be one of her last looks at the sunset over the beach. This had been her favourite time of the day since she'd first arrived. The sun went down quickly. The light changed from intense to subtle and then to black in mere minutes. Trees and boats were silhouetted against the pale blue of the sky. A gentle breeze played off the waves.

She found a chair and sat down, resting her elbows on the table and her head in her hands. So peaceful. It belied everything that had been going on during the day, she thought, and everything that was going on in her head. There was something she had to work out. Richard had confirmed her belief that Jamie Dixon was a no-good philanderer. But did that mean he was a liar too? Had he been truthful with her those five years back? Had Greg really been playing with her affections? Did it matter? Was it too late anyway?

A noise behind her made her turn and both she and the newcomer were startled into recognition.

'Susannah, I need to talk to you ....'

'Greg, I've got something to tell you .....'

As he approached, Susannah could sense some hesitancy about him. He didn't look the poised, self-assured Greg she used to know. He looked ... she couldn't quite put her finger on it. But if she had been pushed to describe him, Susannah was shocked to discover that she would have had to say that he looked remorseful. Surely not?

'Susannah, please, let me say what I have to.' He paused. Again a look of uncertainty crossed his face. Susannah nodded and he sat down opposite her. 'I have to thank you,' he said, once again surprising her. What for, she thought? Running off with Clive Channing as he imagines?

'Why?' The words came out softly. She could see he was having a hard time explaining himself. She couldn't really be angry with him. It was she who had to apologise, for taking Jamie Dixon's word five years ago and running out on him without an explanation. She had certainly had no choice but to respond to the emergency of her father's shooting. But she had expected Greg to get in touch at some point. The course leaders would have told him what had happened. If he had cared anything for her, surely he would have contacted her, if only to see how her father was.

But there had been nothing. Jamie had known what had happened. He had been there when she had been told about her father. Hadn't he said something to Greg? But what?

'Jamie Dixon.'

'What?'

Greg's question jolted Susannah into realising she had spoken the name out loud.

'Nothing. Sorry, Greg. What were you saying?'

'I was trying to thank you, for sorting things out with my father. We had a long talk last night, the best talk we've had in a long time, certainly since John died and probably since my mother died too …' He trailed off into silence.

Susannah could see the emotion getting to him. She wanted desperately to go over and put her arms round him. But he had told her to leave. Her feelings were clearly not reciprocated.

'That's all right, Greg. I'm glad you've sorted things out. He's a lovely man and he's been having a hard time too.'

'I know that now, but only thanks to you.' He paused. 'If only we'd been straight with each other all those years ago.'

Susannah looked up sharply. Was he talking about himself and his father, or about the two of them? Was straight talking the answer now?

'Greg'

'Susannah …'

'This is becoming a habit, sorry.' He stopped and waved his hand, indicating that she should have her say. But Susannah was at a loss for the right words. Did she really want to bring up her suspicions of Jamie Dixon now? If she were wrong, it could reawaken Greg's antagonism towards her. She looked down at her hands to give herself a moment to consider but Greg interrupted her thoughts.

'You mentioned Dixon just now. Did you see him?'

'He's here?' Susannah hoped that Richard had been mistaken. But clearly not.

'Yes, he's here, as patronising and supercilious as ever.'

'I thought he was a friend of yours?' Susannah spoke cautiously. If Greg wasn't that enamoured of Jamie Dixon any more, might there be a chance of sorting out their misunderstanding of five years ago?

'Huh.' Greg looked away from her, out towards the ocean. The sun was sinking and the light fading. 'I thought he was. But I've just found out what a two-faced scumbag he really is!'

The bitterness in his tone was unmistakable and Susannah's hopes soared. She looked at Greg, his profile clear against the subtle tones of the sky. She had never really got over him, she finally admitted to herself. She had fallen for him on the training course and, despite Jamie Dixon's words, she had never stopped loving him, however hard she had tried.

When she was tending her father, life had been difficult and busy. A relationship was probably the last thing she could have coped with. But she remembered the times when she had thought of Greg and wondered why he had never been in touch. Once she had had more time, it was pride that stopped her from contacting him herself.

'What was it that you wanted to tell me?' Greg's voice broke the silence.

She took a deep breath. 'Only that I have another job lined up.'

'What?' Greg almost shouted at her. 'I thought you were going to Boston.' The sharp edge was back in his voice.

'No, Greg. You've got that all wrong.'

'Have I indeed? The two of you looked pretty cosy to me.'

'Yes, it might have looked like that, Greg. But if you had bothered to find out, instead of assuming, I'm sure Clive would have told you himself.'

'Told me what exactly?'

'That he's offered me a job in Boston …'

'Oh, so congratulations are in order, then,' Greg got up quickly, his chair scraping harshly on the flagstones. 'Leave when you like, Susannah. I'll send on what I owe you.'

'I think you owe it to me to listen for a change.' Susannah felt her heart beating fast. This was it. Time for plain speaking. Greg glared at her but stopped in his tracks. Slowly, he turned to face her.

'Well?'

'Well, Clive offered me a job but I turned it down. I told him I couldn't leave here. Africa I mean,' she added quickly as she saw Greg's eyebrows rise. 'So he invited me out there for a holiday, which I accepted.' She paused but hurried on when she thought Greg was about to walk off again. 'But I do have another job lined up, in South Africa. Will that suit you? You didn't want me here in the first place, did you? Well, now you've got your wish and you've even got your mate Jamie right on the spot to step into my shoes.'

'Susannah!' It was cry of anguish from Greg. 'He could never step into your shoes.'

The next moment Susannah found herself lifted from the chair and enveloped in an embrace, Greg holding her gently, and rocking her back and forth.

'Greg?' The words were muffled as Susannah pushed against Greg's chest. He relaxed his hold, guarding her broken arm, but still keeping her in his arms, one hand forcing her chin upwards so she had to meet his eyes.

'I'm sorry, Susannah. I've got to tell you. It was Jamie Dixon who started those rumours about you being a gold-digger.'

Susannah's jaw tightened but she kept quiet.

'I'm to blame because I listened to him. I thought you were after me for my money,' he confessed. 'When you left that night, I never found out why. I never knew about your father until much, much later. Dad told me yesterday that he died earlier this year. I'm so sorry, my love.'

'Greg?' She couldn't believe what she was hearing. What had he just called her? 'Can you ever forgive me?'

'No, I can't, Greg,' she replied and nearly stumbled as he let go of her suddenly. Seeing the look of anguish on his face, she smiled and carried on, 'I can't forgive you because it's not all your fault. I'm just as much to blame.'

'How can that be?'

'Because Jamie Dixon told me that you had girlfriends all over the world and that I was just a distraction for the duration of our course.'

'What?'

'Oh, Greg!' Susannah found she couldn't say any more. There were no more words. Jamie Dixon's deceit had finally been unmasked.

This time when Greg took hold of her, she didn't resist, in fact she welcomed his arms round her waist, putting her one good arm around his neck. Their kiss said more than words ever could and when Susannah pulled away, Greg gently cupped the back of her head to bring her lips back to his. A while later, he released her.

'I have something to ask you,' he said.

'Yes?'

'I don't want you to take that job in South Africa,' his tone was serious, but his eyes were twinkling.

'Oh, really?' Susannah replied, her heart beating fast yet again.

'Yes, really,' the deep blue eyes held hers. 'I've a far better one right here for you, my darling. Not as my assistant manager but as my wife!'

Printed in Great Britain
by Amazon

46726391R00108